MR. GEDRICK AND ME

MR. GEDRICK AND ME

PATRICK CARMAN

KT KATHERINE TEGEN BOOKS
An Imprint of HarperCollins Publishers

Katherine Tegen Books is an imprint of HarperCollins Publishers.

Mr. Gedrick and Me
Copyright © 2017 by Patrick Carman
All rights reserved. Printed in the United States of America.
No part of this book may be used or reproduced in any manner whatsoever
without written permission except in the case of brief quotations embod-
ied in critical articles and reviews. For information address HarperCollins
Children's Books, a division of HarperCollins Publishers, 195 Broadway,
New York, NY 10007.
www.harpercollinschildrens.com

Library of Congress Control Number: 2017932880
ISBN 978-0-06-242160-9

Typography by Joel Tippie
17 18 19 20 21   CG/LSCH   10 9 8 7 6 5 4 3 2 1
❖
First Edition

For Sierra. May your journey lead you home.

Can I Get a Hello?

My name's Stanley. Stanley Darrow.

Lifting weights was my new thing. Curling five-pound dumbbells was no problem, I'd done that plenty of times. But I couldn't lift the bar on the old bench press in the garage. I knew this because I'd tried once already and it got stuck on my chest. The only way I could get out from under the crazy thing was to slide off the bench and land on the garage floor. I kicked the bench hard enough to make my toe hurt. *Note to self:* don't weight lift wearing flip-flops.

But it was summer, and I always wore flip-flops in the summer. I was thinking about all this, wishing my dad were still here to spot me, when I walked into the kitchen searching for some help.

"I'm going out into the garage to lift weights," I told Mom. I did a couple of arm stretches and waited for her to respond, but she didn't say anything. I looked around the kitchen, piled with dirty dishes, and tried to get her attention one more time.

"There's a very good chance I will die out there," I said.

I could see on her face that she noticed I existed. It's like she thought she heard the sound of a voice, but it registered in her busy brain like a woodpecker banging on the refrigerator door.

"That's nice, honey. Have a good time. Oh, and feed Bob while you're out there."

I rolled my eyes and gave it one last shot.

"I'm riding my bike to the store so I can buy ten pounds of candy. And I'm not wearing my helmet."

"Okay, have fun," Mom said. My mom—her name is Elsa—leaned forward, typing something into her laptop with one hand while holding a pencil in the other. Her blond hair fell forward on her face, her small shoulders curving toward the screen. She rested her elbows on the table.

Ever since Dad died and summer vacation showed up, Mom worked from home instead of her big office in downtown Chicago. She's an architect. Her boss, Huxley Harvold, had recently handed her a gigantic project and she had fallen behind on it. I guess I didn't really blame her for ignoring me. She had a lot going on. It was Dad who had clipped the lawn and kept out the weeds. It was Dad who had taken care of the stuff around the house, including me and my brother and sister. Now Mom had to do all that stuff by herself. Her cell phone rang and she groaned before tapping the screen. I decided I better load up on water before heading out for all that candy, so I got a glass and turned on the tap.

"No, no, not to worry, Mr. Harvold. It's all coming along beautifully. The community arts center will be a showpiece, just like you asked."

Mom was out of her chair now, pacing back and forth nervously.

I imagined Huxley Harvold sitting in his office with a big, fat smile on his face. He probably had his feet up on the desk while he pressured Mom to hurry up and get all this work done. I'd been to his office before. The guy's got a very large, heavy-looking desk—it's like a slab of pavement on four legs. He's a little demanding, Huxley.

"Well, no, I don't have anything I can show you yet," Mom said. "But it's really starting to take shape."

Pause pause pause.

"I'll keep at it. Thank you for checking in, Mr. Harvold. Bye for now."

Mom hung up the phone and stared at a big, blank piece of paper sitting on the kitchen table.

"This community arts center is going to kill me," she said.

I could tell she wanted to cry, because the paper was blank and the house was a mess and she missed my dad. Before, she could come home from work, enjoy a nice dinner Dad had made, and then have the energy to help out with things like lifting weights.

She started tapping her pencil on the side of her head, a habit she had when she felt nervous or upset.

I walked down the hallway on the shaggy carpet and peeked into a bedroom. My brother, Fergus, was lying on his bed eating potato chips and watching something on a laptop. I could tell by the sound that it was some kind of baseball highlights reel. Fergus was wearing a White Sox cap, pulled down low to cover half of his face. Also, did I mention my brother is super athletic and very tall, everything I'm not?

"What do you want, dork?" my brother said.

"Good morning to you, too," I replied. I punched the air, warming up my arms for the big lift I was planning.

"Mom says you're supposed to feed Bob and help me do bench presses," I said.

"I doubt that," Fergus answered. He tapped on some keys and looked up. "Are you going to stand there all day? I'm kind of busy here."

Another video started playing and Fergus went back to ignoring me. There was a Nerf football on the floor, halfway hidden under a pile of clothes.

"Why are you entering my room?" Fergus said as I stepped forward and reached down into the glob of clothing.

"This is my football," I said as I picked it up. "Wanna play?"

I threw the ball right at Fergus's head and he caught it without even looking up.

"Man, you are really good at catching stuff," I said.

"Beat it," Fergus replied. His eyes stayed glued to the computer as he threw the football over my head, and it went sailing out the door into the hallway.

I took off running for the ball, but by the time I found it and came back, the door was closed.

"No problem," I yelled. "I'll just play catch with myself, because that's loads of fun."

I spiked the football on the carpet and did an end-zone dance I'd been working on, but there was no one to see me do it. Five more steps down the hallway and I was standing in front of my sister's room. I knocked and she didn't answer, so I knocked again.

"I know you're in there. I can hear you thinking."

"Enter at your own risk," my sister, Amelia, said. Her voice sounded far away.

Amelia's answer was code for *I'm in the middle of drawing and if you come in here I will throw my pencil at you. If it hits you in the eye, don't say I didn't warn you.*

I decided it would be safer to leave the door shut and just yell at her.

"Mom says you're supposed to feed Bob and help me do bench presses!"

There was a long pause and then I heard a huffing sound drift under the door. It swung open and there stood my sister—twelve years old with long blond hair and big eyes just like Mom's. Amelia looked like a smaller version of my mom, right down to the pencil she held in her hand, tapping it against her head.

"If you're lying to me I'm going to hang you upside down from your window and drop you."

My house was all on one floor, so I would only fall about three inches. It sounded fun.

"Yeah, let's do that!" I said. I tried to run to her window, but she was blocking my way.

Amelia looked down at me because she's taller than I am. She pointed her pencil in my face like a magician's wand.

"Abracadabra!" she said.

I stared at her like an idiot.

"This is the part where you disappear," Amelia said. "That's how the trick works."

"A magic show, cool! How does it work? Can you cut me in half or turn me into a goat?"

Amelia's expression didn't change, but the pencil got a little closer to my face. I figured I better change tactics.

"Hey, I can help you with your art project," I said, peering into the room and seeing her drawing pad. "I help you, you help me. It's a win-win."

"You remember what happened last time you helped me on an art project?" Amelia asked. "You kept smudging the paper with your fingers and breaking all my pencils. I had to start all over."

"Yeah, but I've been practicing. I can really draw now. I'm a regular Van Gobble."

Amelia shut the door in my face.

"It's Van *Gogh*," she yelled from behind the door.

I shoved my hands in my pockets and didn't move. What a bunch of selfish dweebs my brother and sister were. How was I supposed to turn my noodle arms into serious guns if no one would help me? It was impossible! So I decided to take Mom up on her offer to buy ten pounds of candy instead.

But first I had to feed Bob.

A Detour and a Strange Encounter

Bob is green, he's got big eyes, and he's got a horn sticking out of his head. He's a lizard. Bob is not one of those giant ones that looks like it might eat your fingers off. He fits in the palm of my hand.

"I don't suppose you could lift that bar off my chest if I'm pinned under it, could you?"

Bob blinked.

"I didn't think so."

I opened a cardboard box that had crickets inside and one of them jumped out.

"It's your lucky day," I said to the escaping cricket. Then I had second thoughts. "Unless you get run over by a car."

Another one jumped out, and Bob watched it sail by and hit the floor in the garage with a *plink*. That was how it usually went when I fed Bob. I always lost a couple of crickets before I could get ahold of one and drop it into Bob's cage. The two crickets that escaped the jaws of death hopped away and I tossed a third one into the cage. Bob's eyes narrowed and he moved one of his legs in super slow motion, turning toward the cricket. It could take five seconds or five hours for Bob to eat his lunch, so I snapped on my bike helmet. There's no sense risking a head injury that might limit my candy intake down the road.

I always think about my dad when I ride my bike through the neighborhood. The two of us used to go on a lot of rides together, but they were never just rides.

"Ready?" my dad would say when we were out of the driveway.

"Born ready!" I would yell, and he'd start pedaling faster.

Then my dad would lead me on a winding pathway through the park. He'd jump off his bike and leap through the chains on the swing set, then get back on his bike and ride over to the slide. Up the slide my dad would go, flying down and getting on his bike again, heading for the monkey bars.

"Is that the fastest you can go?" I would say as I

reached the monkey bars first and started swinging.

"Hey, how'd you pass me? That's impossible!" my dad would say.

And on and on it would go, through a long and twisty course we'd created over a whole summer. I didn't win every time, but it was always close. And afterward, we never failed to get ice cream.

I thought about those days as I rode toward the store, and somewhere along the way, I took a wrong turn. I don't even remember doing it. I cried a little and the wind made the tears run along the side of my face until I wiped them away. After a while I arrived someplace I wasn't expecting to go, and it wasn't to get ten pounds of candy.

There was a metal fence all painted black that ran along the sidewalk, and behind that, headstones. They were in lots of different shapes. Some of them had square tops, some were rounded, some had fancy curves. There were big ones and small ones, old ones weathered by rain and wind, and others that looked like they'd only been there for a few weeks. I rode my bike through the entrance and stayed on the wide path. No one was around but me and the trees and the headstones. The wind blew through the leaves and made a sound like rain hitting pavement.

When I came to a big elm tree I turned the corner and saw the bench I like to sit on, the one that has a good view of where they buried my dad. It's a really nice spot. There are lots of trees and green grass between all the headstones. I stopped short and rolled my bike back so I was hidden behind the elm tree.

Someone was sitting on my bench. It wasn't technically *my* bench, but it still bothered me that someone was sitting there. I could only see the person from behind as he stared into the cemetery. He was wearing a fancy green jacket that looked like pool table felt. A bright white collar peeked out from the edge of the jacket.

"Who is this guy?" I wondered out loud. "And why is he sitting on my bench?"

A leaf started falling from a tree overhead, drifting down toward the man in the green jacket. I wished it was bird poop instead and that it would land right on his green-pool-table-felt shoulder. When the leaf was a few feet over his head, the man jumped up and stood in front of the bench. With the speed of a ninja he took something from his pocket that looked like a silver pen, but then he pulled his arms apart and the pen extended until it was about four feet long. I'm not making this up—he caught the leaf on the end of the pointer while the leaf was falling through the air. He tossed the leaf into the air, caught it on the end of the pointer again, and flipped it over his head. Then he danced with the leaf, keeping it aloft as it rolled around in the air, falling and rising and falling again. Another leaf fell from the tree, and then another, and as they reached him he stabbed each one like the pointer was a fencing sword.

As he did these things I saw that the man was wearing a vest, a white shirt, and a red tie. I couldn't make out his face from where I stood, but I could see he had dark hair. He removed the leaves, retracted the pointer, and put the pointer back in his coat pocket. And then he walked away.

"That was weird," I said.

I decided to turn around and go home.

Help? What Kind of Help?

When I got home, Mom was in the kitchen arguing
with my sister.

"Why can't Fergus do it? He's so lazy," Amelia said.
She was throwing her arms around in the air, which
is something she does when she gets excited or angry.

"Because it's not his turn to do the laundry. It's
your turn," Mom said. "Also, you should spend less
time in your room. It's beautiful outside. Draw on the
patio or in the yard."

"Why don't *you* go outside and draw in the backyard?" Amelia asked sarcastically.

Lately my sister was having a hard time thinking
before she said something rotten. I think it's a girl

thing, but I could be wrong about that. Either way, I wanted to see who would win the fight, so I leaned against the wall and pretended I was watching a movie.

Mom closed her eyes and counted slowly. She'd been trying to calm down more since moving her office from a swanky downtown building to the kitchen table.

"That's it, Mom, go to your quiet place," I said.

"Zip it, Stanley!" Amelia said. Her arms flailed in my direction.

"I have work to do," Mom said when she opened her eyes. "I need all these things—my laptop and my calculator and this big table and all this blank paper."

"It doesn't matter where I sit, Mom!" Amelia shouted. I could tell she was about to start crying and it made her even angrier.

Fergus walked into the kitchen with his hands stuffed into the pockets of his shorts. "When's lunch?"

"Fergus, not now," Mom said with the flat tone of plywood.

Fergus looked back and forth between Mom and Amelia. He realized he'd stepped right into the middle of a cage match in progress, but that wasn't going to stop my brother on the never-ending quest for food. "Are you thinking ten minutes, twenty? Because I have baseball practice later and I really need to eat so my energy level is up."

Fergus mimed like he was swinging a baseball bat and watching a ball soar over a fence.

"Hey, I'll make you a sandwich," I said, springing forward onto my toes. "I love making sandwiches."

"Stanley, you are not making your brother's lunch," Mom scolded. "He's not four years old. He can make his own sandwich."

"Who am I to deprive poor Stanley of practicing his culinary skills?" Fergus argued. "Of course he can make my sandwich."

"Fergus!" Mom yelled. She closed her eyes and started counting again. When her eyes opened up a few seconds later, I was at the refrigerator getting out the mayo and the lunch meat.

"Can you get a ride to practice?" Mom asked. "I'm way behind on this project."

Fergus looked at the blank paper.

"Looks like progress to me."

"Ha ha," Mom said.

"I'm going to my room," Amelia yelled. She stormed out and I counted to three on my own. That's usually how long it takes for her door to slam shut. *One, two, three—BAM!*

Fergus kicked the floor. "So about that lunch?"

Mom looked like her head was going to explode,

but she answered in a very quiet voice. "The refriger-ator is right there. Make a sandwich."

"Already on it!" I said. "Triple-decker Stanley spe-cial, coming right up."

"It's cool," Fergus said. "I'll get a ride. No big deal."

Fergus sulked back to his room. My big brother wasn't so much angry as sad. He probably couldn't imagine this being the new norm around the house, but maybe it was. Dad had been gone for six months—time to get used to it.

"Wanna split a triple-decker Stanley special?" I asked Mom.

She let out a big breath and slumped in her chair. "I'm not hungry, but you enjoy that. It looks delicious."

I thought about getting back on my bike and riding to the store for all the candy I could carry. Or maybe I could go searching for the man in the green jacket. I couldn't stop thinking about the way he'd made those leaves dance around. I thought about learning a trick like that and showing it to my family. Maybe then I could get some attention. I put all the stuff away, poured a glass of milk, and wrapped my sand-wich in a napkin.

"I'm starting to think we might need a little help around here," Mom said.

"Help?" I asked. Mom looked really tired. "What kind of help?"

Mom shrugged and pulled up a web browser. She pushed her long hair behind her ears and let out a deep breath. I took an enormous bite of my sandwich.

"I've been seeing this search return at the top of the list all morning," she said.

"What have you been searching for?" I garbled through a mouthful of sandwich.

Mom paused like she didn't want to say, and then she spoke in a whisper like only she and I could know. *"Nannies."*

"Nannies?" I shouted. Some of my sandwich flew out of my mouth and bounced off Mom's shoulder.

"I feel like we've talked about this," she said, ticking off lessons on her fingers. "Don't put so much food in your mouth at one time, but if you do, make sure you don't talk."

"Right," I said as I tried to choke down another huge chunk of white bread and turkey that was bigger than a baseball. "Smaller bites. Got it."

I swallowed what was left and slugged down half a glass of milk. A burp was crawling up my throat, but somehow I managed to keep my mouth closed while it blew up in my head and exited through my nose. "Seriously, a *nanny*? You mean like a person who lives in our house and makes us food and does our laundry?"

"I guess so," Mom said. She sure seemed exhausted

and stressed and confused. Sometimes it was like she didn't know *what* she was thinking.

I wondered what it might be like to have some help. A nanny? It sounded like someone was going to replace my dad. It didn't seem like a great idea. Then again, I thought maybe this nanny person could also be a bodybuilder and they'd help me lift weights. It could happen.

The listing at the top of Mom's search page was very simple. It said:

Mr. Gedrick of Swoghollow. Cleaning, cooking, caretaking.

"Sounds strange," I said. "And it's a guy. Aren't nannies supposed to be girls?"

"Girls can be anything they want to be," Mom said. "So guys can be mannies."

I thought a manny sounded hilarious and couldn't stop laughing. Whenever I laugh like that, Mom starts laughing, too. She giggled and moved the pointer on the screen. "Let's see where the link goes."

Mom clicked on the link and a page appeared. It, too, was very unusual. There was a fancy logo in the shape of a *G* with swirlies around it. And there was a place to enter an address. That's all.

"You're not seriously going to put our address in there?" I asked. "What if this nanny is an ax murderer?"

But I looked at Mom and felt bad for her. Her hair was all over the place. She hadn't put any makeup on. She was wearing a wrinkled T-shirt that said *Keep Calm and Eat Cookies* on it. She shook her head a few times and ran off to the bathroom.

I tried to eat the rest of my sandwich, but I'd lost my appetite so I dropped it in the trash can. While Mom was gone, I sat down and looked at the page. I felt sorry for myself. I felt sorry for Mom and my brother and my sister. I even felt sorry for Bob and the crickets. Everyone just seemed lonely.

So I did something I probably shouldn't have.

I entered our address in the box on the screen and hit send.

When the screen refreshed, it was completely empty except for five little words.

Help is on the way.

I closed out of the browser and said a little prayer.

Please let him cook like a champ. And let him be really good at weight lifting.

Timbuktu and a Kangaroo

I think I'll talk about my dad now. He was what some people call a Mr. Mom, so I guess he might have made a pretty good manny, now that I think about it. But I never saw my dad as a Mr. Mom. More like he was my friend and my teacher. And he was really encouraging. I miss that the most, I think.

"Have you ever heard of a place called Timbuktu?" he asked us kids a while back, when we were all younger.

"That's not a real place," we all said. "Is it?"

"Oh, it's real. I'll show you. It's right there."

He showed it to us on a big globe he kept in the garage. The globe was so big, if any of us could have opened it up, we could have lived inside of it. We could have put beds in there and a couch and a TV and a bunch of bananas and stayed in there for a month. Maybe it wasn't *that* big, but none of us could get our arms all the way around it. So it wasn't small.

Dad talked all about invaders and relics and golden ages and we were suddenly big fans of Timbuktu. We could tell he was just as excited by the way he talked, waving his arms around as his voice got louder and he talked faster. Like I said before, Amelia does this, too, just like my dad used to. She loves throwing her arms around while she talks.

Sometimes the places my dad would tell us about didn't seem real at all. Magical places with giant bunnies and big, open plains. But then we got older and realized that Australia probably was a real place and that kangaroos acted a lot like giant bunnies. My brother and my sister didn't care about stuff like this anymore, but I did. I still wondered sometimes if the places Dad told me about were real, or if maybe some of them were made up. Or if some of them were magic places, because sometimes he talked about unicorns and that didn't seem possible.

But I wished and wished anyway. I wished that some kind of magic would arrive and put my family back together. I left the kitchen and went to the garage, where I spun the big globe like I used to. I felt the smooth surface of the globe run along my palm. I listened to it spin on its axis, squeaking as it moved in a circle. It's heavy, so once you get it going, it turns for a long time. I thought about my dad and the garage felt very empty. Everything was quiet by the time the globe stopped.

I closed my eyes and pointed to a place on the globe, just like I did with my dad. He would tell me all about whatever place I'd pointed to. As I opened my eyes in the garage and moved in real close, I squinted so I could read the tiny type. I pointed to a city or a town, I wasn't sure which. It was on a big continent and it was all alone: *Swoghollow.*

"Where have I heard that name before?" I asked myself.

I stared at it for a minute, and then I let my hand fall to my side and looked around the garage where Dad's imagination used to take up so much space. I heard a cricket chirp. I made a promise then—from the bottom of my flip-flops to the top of my Chicago Cubs baseball cap—that I would find a way to put my family back together again.

Now if only I had a clue about how I was going to do it.

Mr. Gedrick of Swoghollow

Six hours later, my family was sitting at the dinner table staring at the food. We were eating frozen pizza, and there was a big bowl of uneaten broccoli sitting next to Fergus. He passed it to his left, knowing it would be just as full when it came back around.

"So what did everyone do today?" Mom asked. She wasn't very good at small talk. She took a bite of her pizza and realized it was burned on the bottom.

"I fed Bob," I said. "And I rode over and visited Dad."

That got everyone's attention.

"What a nice thing to do," Amelia said. But there was an edge to her voice, I thought because it made her feel guilty for not visiting the cemetery more often. I didn't think she'd been there in months. She dropped a half-eaten piece of pizza on her plate and went to her room.

"I'm not eating her share of the broccoli," Fergus said. "No way."

"Was it something I said?" I asked.

Fergus shook his head like I should have known better. "She's sensitive, remember?"

"Yeah but—"

"Don't worry about it, little bro," Fergus cut me off, stuffing pizza in his mouth. "Women are a mystery."

Mom looked at Fergus like he was four years old and didn't have a clue.

Then the doorbell rang.

"Are you expecting someone?" Mom asked. She looked back and forth between Fergus and me.

"Not me," I said.

"Nope," Fergus mumbled. I could tell he hoped one of his baseball buddies was coming by to rescue him from the morgue that had become his home.

For a while after Dad died a lot of the nosy neighbors dropped by with casseroles and plates of cookies. Dad had been friendly with all the moms, but Mom went into Chicago every day for work. She left early and got home late. I think some of the other moms thought she worked too much. They might have wondered if Mom could handle us without my dad. After all, he was the one who fed us and got us off to school on time and mowed the lawn. I think Mom was happy when the free food and the advice stopped showing up.

We all went to the door. Who would come see us out of the blue? Even Amelia came out of her room, holding a tissue and sniffling. The house was in shambles, and looking around, I hoped the visitor wouldn't want to come inside.

"Whoever it is, they're getting quite a welcome," Mom said as we gathered around her.

She opened the door and my jaw dropped. It might have actually hit the floor.

The strange man from the cemetery was standing on the front porch. He had the same fuzzy green jacket, and up close, it really did look like pool table felt. He had the matching green vest and the white shirt and the red tie. His black hair was perfectly combed, like an old movie star's. He had bright green eyes that gave us a grave look. His pointed nose was a little long for his face, and he was taller than I had realized from a distance when I'd seen him in the cemetery.

"Can I help you?" Mom asked, pushing us back

behind her like she was trying to protect us from a pack of wolves.

"I believe it is I who can help you," the man said. He bowed and stood up straight again. And then he introduced himself and I almost fainted.

"Mr. Gedrick of Swoghollow, at your service."

Something Impossible Happens in the Kitchen

Mom was having a momentary lapse of brain function. Instead of saying *no thank you, we're fine*, and then closing the door on Mr. Gedrick, she allowed him to take one step into the house. And then another. Before she knew it he had his retractable pointer out at full length, poking at a sock stuck on top of the ceiling fan. He pulled it down with the pointer.

"Size eleven, white," he said. Then he sniffed it. "Baseball field."

"Maybe that's mine," Fergus said, even though he was *sure* it was his. I'd watched him throw it up there weeks ago.

Mr. Gedrick held the sock out in Fergus's direction,

where it sat on the end of the pointer. "I know it's your sock, Fergus. Let's not make a habit of storing it there in the future, shall we?"

Fergus took the sock and stuffed it in his pocket like he had no idea where else to put it. I looked at Mr. Gedrick and wondered: *How does this guy know about my brother's stinky socks?*

Mom was still standing at the door, holding it open like she was getting ready to go somewhere. She blew a strand of blond hair out of her face and it fell right back where it was before.

"Excuse me, Mr. Gedrick, was it?" she asked. "I don't recall sending a message for any help. I'm afraid you must have the wrong house. I'm going to have to ask you to leave."

That was true, Mom hadn't sent for Mr. Gedrick. But I had! Mom was awfully busy, and I could see the wheels turning in her head. Had she requested his services? Maybe she had filled in the blanks without even thinking about it. She nodded her head toward the door as if to say *could you please go find another family to help?* But her face said something different.

Mr. Gedrick paid no attention to my mom. He walked right through the living room, carefully moving around backpacks and piles of old homework and empty pizza boxes. As he passed by the remote control for the television set, he tapped it with his pointer and the TV turned off.

"Hey, I was watching that," Fergus said. Then he seemed to remember that no, he had actually been eating dinner. "I mean I was *going* to watch that. Turn it back on."

"How much baseball can one person stand?" Amelia asked.

"I'm sure you'd rather watch a dance competition," Fergus yelled.

"If it saves us all from a bunch of idiots running around in circles with sticks in their hands, yes!" Amelia fired back.

Fergus shook his head and let out a snort. "For starters, they don't carry anything around the bases," Fergus said as he walked over and picked up the remote. "And it's not a stick, you nitwit, it's a bat."

Mom put her hand on her forehead and stared at the floor, shaking her head. This was getting embarrassing.

I could tell Amelia was about to lay into Fergus but Mom looked up and cut her off.

"Mr. Gedrick, I really do need you to leave."

Mr. Gedrick seemed to me like someone who had been in situations like this before, a guy who was observing everything but acting like he wasn't. He busied himself looking at the ceiling, then the doorway to the kitchen, and then the hallway that led to my dad's old study and the bedrooms. He retracted the pointer and placed it back into his pocket. When his hand came back out he was holding a small booklet, which he opened. I peeked over and saw the cover: *Field Guide, Darrows*. Maybe he thought we were a family of birds. A pen found its way into his other hand and he began jotting down notes.

"Hey, the dang TV won't turn on," Fergus said, his frustration building.

"Good," Amelia grumbled as she sat down on the couch. She stood right back up again and picked up one of my Star Wars action figures. "Stanley, I swear, if you don't stop leaving these butt zappers lying around I'm going to hit them all with a hammer."

"Butt zappers, good one," I said. Amelia threw the toy at my head and missed by a mile.

"You're really out of practice," I said. "Wanna play catch later?"

Amelia huffed and sank back down into the couch. But I could tell she was just as curious as everyone else about this strange person standing in our house. She kept her eye on Mr. Gedrick.

"Amelia, calm down," Mom said. She shut the front door so the entire neighborhood couldn't hear all the yelling. I wondered if the neighbors were worried about us. Or maybe they were just curious? Mom eyed Fergus. "The last thing we need is a baseball game right now. Everyone be quiet while I figure this out."

She turned to where Mr. Gedrick had been standing and started to say something, but then she noticed that he was gone. It was very strange—one second he was there, and the next he wasn't.

"Which way did he go?" Mom asked, looking at each of us one at a time.

"What is up with this TV?" Fergus complained. He kept pointing the remote and hitting all the buttons like he was firing a laser gun.

"He must have gone down the hallway!" I said.

Fergus and Amelia looked at each other like they were going to start arguing again. But they both shrugged—a silent truce. I led the charge toward the back of the house and everyone followed me. We found Mr. Gedrick peering into one room after another, taking notes in his field guide.

"Mr. Gedrick," Mom said pleadingly, approaching him slowly like he was a dog that had wandered in and might snap at one of us.

"A moment, if you please," Mr. Gedrick said as he wrote with impressive speed. He finished whatever he was jotting down and walked right into Amelia's room.

"Hey!" Amelia shouted. "You can't go in there. That's my room!"

Everyone arrived at her door at the same time and tried to jam in close so we could see what was going on. Mr. Gedrick was standing at the window, staring outside. There was something sad about the way he gazed out into the yard. He turned in our direction, raised a dark eyebrow, and the doorbell rang.

"You've gotta be kidding me," Mom said.

I could already imagine Mrs. Tingman or Mrs. Fleewert from down the street standing on our porch asking if everything was okay. The last thing Mom needed was a rumor running up and down the streets about a man in a green felt jacket loose in her house. She pointed a finger at Mr. Gedrick. "Don't go anywhere."

While Mom was racing back toward the door, Mr. Gedrick walked right past the rest of us like we weren't even there. I looked at my brother and sister and thought: *useless as usual.* Then I chased after Mr. Gedrick.

"Hmmmm, yes. This will do just fine," Mr. Gedrick said when he arrived at the door to my room.

"It's the best room in the house, for sure," I said. I'm proud of my room, even if it currently looked like a toy and underwear bomb had exploded in a thousand directions.

"This will all have to go," Mr. Gedrick said, sweeping his arm across the space. He looked down his long nose at me and flashed his brilliant green eyes. "I'm afraid you'll need to move in with your brother."

"What!" Fergus yelled.

"Cool!" I said as I looked at my big brother. "What's up, roomie?"

"This is insane," Amelia complained.

Mr. Gedrick walked back to the living room and we all followed him. This was turning out to be one heck of an adventure.

Mom was arguing with someone at the door when Mr. Gedrick showed up behind her. She closed the door partway so she could hide the weirdness taking place in our living room.

"Who's at the door, Mom?" I asked.

Mom glanced back and forth from the front porch to Mr. Gedrick. "Just a neighbor, it's nothing. Why don't you take our guest into the kitchen? A glass of water, maybe?"

Mr. Gedrick's eyebrow went up again and he looked toward our kitchen. He seemed happy about this turn of events, like the kitchen was where he had wanted to go from the moment he'd arrived.

Dirty dishes were piled in the sink. The table was filled with half-eaten food. A second table, in the corner, was covered with Mom's work stuff. The floors were dirty, the counters were cluttered, and the garbage can was overflowing. Mr. Gedrick frowned when his eyes landed on a teetering stack of pizza boxes on the floor.

"Oh my," Mr. Gedrick said. He lowered his head and surveyed the situation. It looked like he was forming a battle plan.

"It's his turn to clean the kitchen," I said, pointing at Fergus.

Fergus lowered his gaze on me. "Zip it, nerd."

Mr. Gedrick had his pointer out again and as he moved around the kitchen he started picking things up. First it was a dishrag flipped up and over his head. It landed in Amelia's hand. Then the little pantry door with the cleaning supplies opened and the mop flew out. Did Mr. Gedrick pick it up and throw it or did it take flight by itself? I had no idea as the mop landed in Fergus's hands. The water turned on at the sink and Mr. Gedrick kicked a little bench over where I could stand and help with the dishes. Mr. Gedrick glanced at me and nodded.

"Everyone get busy," he said. "This shouldn't take more than a pinch and a twist."

"A pinch and a twist?" I asked as Fergus wet the mop in the sink.

"Or maybe a twist and a pinch," Mr. Gedrick answered offhandedly. "We shall see."

Mr. Gedrick looked toward the front door and nodded once, then he returned to his work.

Mom had finally succeeded in sending the neighbor away. I could see her coming toward the kitchen when the doorbell rang again.

"This can't be happening," she said. "I'll get it!"

In the kitchen, the dishes were flying by as Mr. Gedrick washed them and I dried them and the floor was getting mopped and the counters were being scrubbed. It all happened so fast that none of us had time to complain. Mr. Gedrick pulled out two fresh trash bags as I fell behind on the drying, and in no time flat, all the garbage on the counters was packed up and the bags were tied shut and set on the back porch.

Fergus finished mopping, or the mopping finished Fergus, I couldn't say which. It was like he only hung on to the mop and it was twirling him around the kitchen. The floors had never sparkled so brightly. The mop was put away and everyone dashed to the sink to finish the dishes.

Something weird was going on here. I kept glancing at Fergus and Amelia and I could tell they felt the same way. They couldn't believe the kitchen was suddenly as clean as it had ever been, but they also couldn't help but smile at the result. Was it magic, or was it a pinch and a twist, like Mr. Gedrick had said? One thing was for sure: I was starting to like whatever shenanigans Mr. Gedrick had brought to my house.

The kitchen was spotless, but Mr. Gedrick went around one more time as we stood together and watched—he nudged the toaster a little straighter, wiped a small smudge on the refrigerator door, and turned to us. He put his finger to his lips and made the *shhhhhhhh* sound, like we were all in on some big secret. And then he winked with one of those bright green eyes of his and for the first time I saw him smile. It wasn't a big smile; it was a small crafty one, just at the corner of his mouth. He was pleased with himself. And, I thought, pleased with his helpers.

That's when Mom arrived in the kitchen.

"We helped!" I yelled, because it seemed like the right thing to say.

Mom had walked into the kitchen ready to drag Mr. Gedrick outside by his red tie if she had to, but then she became more confused than ever. Mom loved tidy things, like her beautiful office in downtown Chicago. She'd missed this kind of order and precision, I could tell. But how in the world did it happen? She pinched herself, maybe wondering if she had been asleep and dreaming at her table. She twisted all around, looking in every direction.

"You see there," Mr. Gedrick said. "A pinch. And a twist."

I thought this was amazing and I smiled like when I figure out a tough math problem all on my own.

Mom didn't seem to know what to say. Her life had recently been turned upside down, and here it was being tumbled in a dryer all over again.

"Children," Mr. Gedrick said. "Might I have a moment alone with your mother?"

Fergus got a stern look on his face, like he was the man of the house.

"You two go ahead," Fergus said to me and Amelia. "I'll keep an eye on things here."

Amelia glared at Fergus. She wasn't going to be pushed around, not by a baseball-loving nincompoop like Fergus.

"Come on, Amelia," I said, pulling her toward the hall. "Let's go move all my stuff into Fergus's room!"

This was the cruelest thing she could do to her older brother, so she followed me out of the kitchen.

I stopped short in the living room as Fergus asked Mr. Gedrick a question.

"If I turn the TV back on, will it work?"

"I don't see why not," Mr. Gedrick answered with a twinkle in his eye. "Is there something wrong with it?"

Fergus backed slowly into the living room until he was standing right next to me. "I'm going to be sitting right here, Mom. And I'll have my baseball bat."

"I don't think a baseball bat will help with the television set," Mr. Gedrick said.

Fergus eyed Mr. Gedrick warily and kept backing

up, and then he was sitting on the couch. He decided not to go to his room and get the baseball bat after all.

The TV came back on and all three of us inched our way back toward the kitchen door. There was no way we were going to miss this. We hid there so we could hear what they were saying.

"Look, Mr. Gedrick, I don't know what to tell you," Mom started. She didn't seem to know what to say. "This is all very confusing. How did you even find us?"

"*You* found *me*," Mr. Gedrick said like Mom was being totally dense. "Obviously."

Mom didn't understand this, but I did.

"You can't expect to live here with us. We haven't even talked about how much that would cost."

Mr. Gedrick slowly reached out his green-sleeved arm and handed Mom some papers.

"All the appropriate background checks and references," Mr. Gedrick said.

She looked through the material and seemed satisfied.

"I know how hard things have been for you," Mr. Gedrick said, lowering his arm and placing both hands in the pockets of his felt jacket. "For the time you need me, I can shoulder some of the burden. I can help if only you'll let me, and my price is surprisingly reasonable. We can work all that out later."

Mom seemed to think and think and think. She didn't say a word. After about ten seconds she nodded ever so slightly.

"Your things are on the front porch," she said. "Someone left them there, though I told them not to."

"Ah yes, my things," Mr. Gedrick said excitedly. "I'll have that all cleaned up before I make your evening tea. Not a problem."

"My evening tea?" Mom asked.

"Well, of course," Mr. Gedrick said. "But first I need to get Fergus to practice and then I will put my things in order. It won't take more than a splish and a splash."

"A splish and a splash?" Mom said.

Mr. Gedrick went toward the living room and found us all standing next to the door. "Fergus, you'll be late. Better get your glove and meet me out front."

"I already have a ride," Fergus said. "And you don't have a car."

"Nonsense," Mr. Gedrick replied. "I've canceled your ride and my car will be arriving momentarily."

I didn't see how Mr. Gedrick could have canceled my brother's ride, but then again, he'd just helped us clean the kitchen in four minutes flat. Fergus looked at Mom.

"You okay with this?"

Mom seemed to have changed her mind about Mr. Gedrick, as she shrugged.

"I suppose so," she said.

Mr. Gedrick followed Fergus down the hall, where Fergus threw a fit as I jumped up and down on his bed. He grabbed his glove and baseball shoes and yelled at me. "Don't touch any of my stuff, wimp!"

Mr. Gedrick looked at me. I think maybe he knew he could trust me. "How about you come with us? You can tidy all this up when we return."

"No problem!" I said.

And that's how it all began with Mr. Gedrick.

It would get a lot weirder before the summer was over.

FRED

Apparently while Fergus was putting on his baseball shoes, Mr. Gedrick's car showed up in our driveway. I wished I could have seen it drive up, but I was too busy following Mr. Gedrick around the house, wondering what he would do next. Would there have been a driver? I had no idea! All I knew was what Mr. Gedrick said.

"Fred has arrived. We best not keep him waiting."

"Who's Fred, your driver?" I asked as I tried to pull Fergus up off the floor. My brother was a heavy guy, so I wasn't making any progress.

"You have your own driver?" Fergus asked as he swatted me away and kept tying his baseball shoes.

"Come along, boys," Mr. Gedrick said. "As I've already said. Fred is waiting."

I ran to the front door and pulled it open. Before I could say anything Fergus was next to me on the porch and we were both staring at the driveway.

"That's the dumbest car I've ever seen," Fergus said. "I'm not getting in that thing."

"Oh, but you are," Mr. Gedrick said, glancing at his watch, which had hands that looked like lightning bolts. "In fact, we need to hurry. You're nearly late."

"Where's Fred?" I asked. I looked around the front of the house for a man dressed like a driver.

"Why, he's right there," Mr. Gedrick said as he pointed at the car.

Fred was the smallest automobile I'd ever seen. There were only two seats tightly packed up close to the dashboard, which was made of shiny wood. Fred looked like it was built for a seven-year-old to race around a go-kart track. It was painted bright red and there was no roof.

"I don't think we're all going to fit," I said. "It's too small. But I do like Fred. He's definitely my kind of transportation."

Mr. Gedrick walked over to Fred and popped the tiny trunk. He dug his hands around in there for a while and there were noises like metal bumping against other pieces of metal.

"What are you doing, Mr. Gedrick?" I asked.

He didn't answer me, but a few seconds later he pulled out a little round contraption with two wheels. It didn't seem like it could have fit inside of the trunk, but there it was. Mr. Gedrick carried the round thingamabob to the passenger's side of the car and set it on the pavement. He pulled some tools out of his green felt jacket and started doing some work where I couldn't see. When he stood back up, there was a sidecar attached to Fred's door.

"Whoa! I call dibs on the sidecar!" I yelled. I ran as fast as I could so Fergus couldn't get there first and jumped inside. It was tight, but I totally fit.

Mr. Gedrick went to the driver's side and got in. He started Fred and it sounded like a wimpy lawn mower. Fergus climbed over me and got in on his side. His knees were in his chest. Mr. Gedrick didn't fit much better, and the steering wheel rested on the tops of his knees. Fergus and I watched as Mr. Gedrick strapped on a pair of driving goggles, which made him look even nuttier.

"Are you sure this thing is safe?" Fergus asked, but hearing the sputtering sound of the engine as it warmed up, he laughed. "With an engine like that, it can't possibly do over twenty."

Mr. Gedrick smiled that slight smile in the corner of his mouth and grabbed the stick shift with his long, elegant fingers. "Buckle up and hold on. I believe Fred is in one of his moods."

As soon as Fergus and I snapped our seat belts closed, Mr. Gedrick slammed the gearshift into reverse and Fred bolted from the driveway like a rocket leaving for orbit. A split second later, Fergus and I were thrown back in our seats as Mr. Gedrick switched to first gear and Fred peeled out toward the ballpark.

"This is the best car in the history of cars!" I said.

Fred drove close to the ground, just an inch or two over the pavement, so it felt like going a hundred miles an hour when we made a hard left out of the neighborhood. Fred went up on two wheels and I ended up four feet off the ground as we reached the widest part of the turn, then we crashed back down on all six wheels and wobbled like crazy. We were on the sidewalk for a short distance and Fergus yelled as he saw a woman walking her dog up ahead. The dog and the woman jumped into someone's front yard, but Mr. Gedrick was already back on the road by then, slamming the gear into second, third, and fourth. Fred went up on his back wheels and screeched through an intersection.

"Okay, okay!" Fergus shouted. "I get it! Fred is fast. He's also dangerous!"

"This is awesome!" I yelled.

"You should try sitting here when he's angry," Mr. Gedrick yelled into the driving wind. He shivered like it was a ride we wouldn't want to take. "Be there in a jiffy."

Fergus closed his eyes as we raced through another intersection and swerved around two cars, and when he opened them again, we had arrived at the ballpark.

"There you have it," Mr. Gedrick said as he pushed the goggles up on his forehead. "Tip-top, head to toe."

We'd driven how far? Seven miles? How had we arrived so quickly? Time seemed to bend to the will of Mr. Gedrick.

"I like Fred," I said. "He's my new best friend."

"I'll return at eight p.m. sharp," Mr. Gedrick said, staring up into the sky. He seemed to be marking the location of the sun. "Throw hard, run fast."

These were words I'd heard my dad say to Fergus: *Throw hard, run fast.* I could see Fergus remembering, too, but he shook his head and got out of the car without saying anything about it.

"Ta-ta," Mr. Gedrick said, and the car raced away.

As we made our way back to the house, I wondered how Mr. Gedrick could know those words. It wasn't possible. Dad had said them before every practice and every game.

Mr. Gedrick slowed down, patting the dashboard

like he was trying to soothe a savage beast. Something about seeing the ballpark made his shoulders slump. He took a deep breath and sat taller in the seat.

"You can do this," he said.

"Do what?" I asked from the sidecar. He seemed to have forgotten I was a stowaway on the trip.

"Oh, just encouraging Fred," Mr. Gedrick said, but I didn't think that was true. It sounded to me like he was talking to *himself*. "Let's get you home so you can set up your new room and I can set up mine."

Mr. Gedrick pressed harder on the gas pedal and we sped toward my house.

MR. GEDRICK'S ROOM

By the time Fergus returned home from practice with Mr. Gedrick, his room had been taken over by a nine-year-old boy. And that boy was me!

"How do you like it?" I asked with a big, toothy grin on my face. I was standing on my bed, which I'd shoved right next to Fergus's bed. It was like one giant bed taking up half the room. Getting my bed in there had been almost impossible. It's like ten times bigger than I am. The dang thing had me pinned against the wall twice and I nearly suffocated both times.

"My life is over," Fergus said as he stood in the doorway. He tossed his glove into the closet and leaned heavily against the wall next to the door.

"No way!" I said as I jumped up and down between the two beds. "Look, I brought all my best toys and games and organized them in boxes so they're easy to find. You want Monopoly? I got Monopoly!"

I leapt from the bed and pulled out the game, then placed it carefully back in its spot next to Risk and Sorry!

"And check out these posters!" I said, pointing to the ceiling above the beds. Fergus looked up and saw Star Wars, Wimpy Kid, and Harry Potter posters covering what had once been a sheet of white nothingness.

"I have to admit," Fergus said, "they do liven up the place."

"This is going to be amazing!" I yelled. I was practically jumping out of my underwear I was so excited.

Fergus shook his head. He looked tired from practice and a little freaked out from driving at breakneck speed in a car named Fred.

"Keep your stuff in those boxes and don't touch any of my things," Fergus said. "And stay off my bed."

"No problem, roomie!" I shouted. I couldn't believe my big brother was going to let me stay in his room. I was sure Fergus would pitch a monster fit and throw my stuff out in the hallway.

Fergus sat down on the one chair in our room, the one that goes with the desk piled high with laundry.

"You're going to have to pay rent, you know."

I stopped jumping on my bed. "What kind of rent? I can barely keep up with the baseball cards and candy I need to survive."

Fergus looked around the room and pondered. "Make my bed every morning and do all my laundry. And when I don't feel like it, you do my other chores."

I weighed my options: sleep in the hallway, sleep in my sister's room, or break out the tent and sleep in the backyard. The backyard could be fun, but rooming with Fergus? Way better. I kind of liked chores anyway; they gave me something to do while everyone ignored me. Plus think of all the cool stuff I could do with Fergus now that we were rooming together. How bad could a few chores be?

"You got a deal," I said. "But I'm not folding your underwear."

We shook on it, and then Fergus made me go to the kitchen and get him a soda.

"Why don't you have a glass of water instead?" Mom said when I got to the kitchen and pulled an orange soda out of the fridge.

"It's not for me. It's for Fergus."

Mom's eyes narrowed. "You don't have to get things for him. He's older, but he's not your boss."

That was when the racket started. Mom took the

can of soda from me and we rushed for the hallway. Fergus and Amelia were already standing outside their rooms.

"This day is never going to end," Fergus said.

"Are you hearing this?" Amelia asked.

Fergus walked farther down the hallway, listening carefully. "It's coming from Stanley's old room."

Mom held the can of soda out to Fergus. "Next time get your own drink. Stanley's not your servant."

"Kid needs a work ethic," Fergus said as he popped the top on the can. "Just doing my big brother duty."

Mom rolled her eyes as I crept closer to my old door. We were all standing there, and it struck me that we hadn't been all together in one place very often lately. Strange that it was the hallway we were meeting in, but at least we were together.

"Someone needs to tell him to keep it down in there," Amelia said.

It sounded like Mr. Gedrick was using a bunch of power tools and hammers to build a fort in my old room. I was dying to get a look in there.

We leaned in close.

"Excuse me, Mr. Gedrick?" Mom said in a soft voice. She knocked gently on the door. "I wonder if you might finish, um, whatever it is you're doing in there after everyone is up tomorrow morning. How would that be?"

The noise stopped at the sound of Mom's voice and there was a pause, then Mr. Gedrick opened the door a pinch and looked out. The bright green of his eyeball darted back and forth between all of us, and the door shut again.

"Mr. Gedrick is so weird," I said. "Isn't it great?"

Mom seemed to feel a small surge of motherly competence and it showed on her face as she nodded at all of us. "Let that be a lesson to you. All it takes is good solid communication and things go just as they're supposed to."

No sooner had she said these words than the racket started up again, louder than before.

"This is impossible!" Amelia said. She returned to her room and slammed the door shut.

"Don't anyone else panic," Mom said, but I could tell she was starting to lose her nerve.

"I wonder what he's building in there," I asked. "I bet it's a jungle gym. Or a pool table. Or a water bed!"

"Stanley, you're a dork," Fergus said. He went back to our room, and right before he could shut the door, I somersaulted inside.

"Someone get me a flyswatter. There's a huge, stupid bug crawling around my room!" Fergus screamed.

"Fergus, you are hilarious!" I shouted.

"Shut up, you idiots!" Amelia yelled from down the hall.

Three hours later, the noise from my old room hadn't quieted one bit. About once every hour, one of us went to the door and pounded on it, yelling for Mr. Gedrick to keep it down in there. What followed was a moment of complete silence that lasted about ten seconds. It was like we'd found a wild animal and he had gone totally still, hoping for the intruder to go away. And then, thinking we had gone, the animal would move again. Mr. Gedrick would go right back to sawing and banging.

This went on all night and well into the morning, until finally, at about three a.m., it got very quiet. Everyone was so tired we didn't bother going down the hall to see what the result of all the noise was, and besides, we were afraid if we did Mr. Gedrick would start up again.

It wasn't until seven a.m. sharp the next morning that everyone woke up, not of our own willpower. No, we woke up because we smelled the bacon and the waffles and the coffee.

Bacon and Baseball Stats

We all arrived in the kitchen yawning and rubbing the sleep out of our eyes. We never woke up this early in the morning, especially Amelia and Fergus, who slept past ten a.m. in the summer. Even Mom, who had her work, wouldn't have crawled out of bed for at least another hour, especially with Mr. Gedrick keeping her awake all night. But the smell of bacon sizzling and waffles steaming was so powerful, there was nothing we could do but get up and follow our noses like zombies.

"You snore," I said to Fergus as we arrived in the kitchen.

"Do not," Fergus said.

I shrugged, but I'm pretty sure it was true.

"Must have been Amelia," Fergus added. "She snores like a chain saw."

"Why don't you go back under the rock where you came from," Amelia said.

"Whoa," I said as the arguing was about to go into full swing. "Check it out!"

Mr. Gedrick was wearing an apron that said *Mr. Gedrick's Waffle House. Tips Optional.* The table was covered in a gold-colored cloth and there were bright red place mats and white plates. And in the middle sat a two-foot-tall pile of steaming waffles that looked like it might fall over. There was a plate of crispy bacon, a pot of hot coffee, a jug of milk, and a big bowl of blue and red berries.

"Okay, now I'm awake," Fergus said. He pulled three waffles off the top of the stack and it wobbled back and forth. By the time everyone sat down the stack was cut in half and syrup was being poured and bacon was being crunched.

Mr. Gedrick smiled at the result of his cooking.

"Come join us, Mr. Gedrick," I said, then I bit into the bacon and my mouth exploded with flavor. It was just-right crunchy, with a sweet and salty mix that made my toes tingle.

"No, no, the chef has already eaten," Mr. Gedrick said. "I was up early. Couldn't sleep a wink last night. Someone was snoring."

Everyone laughed. We ate and ate and talked and talked and Mom beamed—it all felt so *normal*.

"Can I see what my old room looks like?" I asked after I'd polished off my fourth waffle.

Mr. Gedrick turned from some work at the sink with one eyebrow raised. He picked up a spatula and tapped it against the palm of his hand.

"I think not," Mr. Gedrick finally said.

"I could just go around the side of the house and look in the window," I said.

"Not advisable," Mr. Gedrick replied as he returned to the dishes. "There might be booby traps out there. Who can say?"

"Booby traps? You mean like in a spy novel? What kind of booby traps?"

Mr. Gedrick's eyes narrowed and he turned toward me. "Not the fun kind."

I shivered, but I also laughed. Besides my dad, I thought Mr. Gedrick was the most mysterious, most unusual, most amazing person ever.

"The Cubs are playing the Nationals at eleven," Fergus said. "Okay if I head over to Ernie's house to watch it?"

Ernie lived seven houses down on the other side of the street. He was a baseball nut like Fergus. They were on the same team.

Mom nodded and grabbed the last piece of bacon before anyone else could get it.

"The Chicago Cubs," Mr. Gedrick said wistfully. "I think Anthony Rizzo will break a hundred RBIs again this year."

Fergus lit up like a Christmas tree. "You know about baseball?"

Mr. Gedrick didn't answer, but Amelia perked right up. She was a whiz with baseball stats and it drove my brother crazy.

"Bryce Harper will give him a run for his money," Amelia said. "He's the next Hank Aaron."

Mr. Gedrick turned to Amelia and peppered her with statistical questions about baseball.

"How many RBIs did the great Hank Aaron have?" Mr. Gedrick asked.

"More than a thousand," I said through a mouthful of waffle. Some syrup dripped down my chin. "I think anyway."

"Two thousand two hundred and ninety-seven," Amelia said offhandedly, like she really didn't care one way or the other.

"That's correct," Mr. Gedrick said. "How about home runs? Who has the most of those?"

"Barry Bonds, seven hundred sixty-two," Amelia said without hesitating. "But that's in the new era, you know, with all the performance-enhancing quackery. I like Willie Mays the best. Six hundred sixty homers."

Fergus's good mood was rapidly being swallowed up by Amelia showing off, so he decided to do some showing off of his own. "So far I've got eleven homers this season, and we've got a bunch of games to go. And I've thrown thirty-eight strikeouts. Double threat."

Amelia rolled her eyes and turned to Mom. "This is why I don't bother coming out of my room."

She took a bowl of berries and stood up, and everyone else got up to leave, too.

Mr. Gedrick stared at Fergus for a long time, and Amelia decided to stay and see where this was going.

"Could you stop eyeballing me?" Fergus said. "It's freaking me out."

"Have you really thrown thirty-eight strikeouts already this year?" Mr. Gedrick asked. He wouldn't stop looking at Fergus, so Fergus lowered his gaze.

"Something like that. Maybe it's more like twenty-eight, I can't really remember."

Mr. Gedrick waited until Fergus looked at him again, and he held his gaze.

"There is nothing more insufferable than a liar.

Don't exaggerate the facts, Fergus. It will only lead to trouble."

"Okay, okay," Fergus said. "You don't have to make such a big deal about it."

"Oh, but I do," Mr. Gedrick said. "You will find, if you haven't already, that a liar is very easy to spot and very much mistrusted. Don't go down that road, not ever."

I could tell Fergus's pride was hurt. I felt sorry for him, but he asked for it. Fergus hates getting caught in a lie, especially in front of me and Amelia.

Amelia smiled sarcastically and shook her head.

"Time to do the dishes," Mr. Gedrick said. "Eight hands are faster than two by one hundred times."

"Is that really true?" I asked. I sensed the possibility of magic showing up in the kitchen again.

"Of course it's not true," Fergus said. "Just ask Amelia. She's the numbers nut."

Amelia glared at Fergus.

"Stanley, you shuttle the dishes over here," Mr. Gedrick said. "Fergus, you're on drying. Amelia, store the extra food. I'll fill in the gaps."

Mom stood up and started to help, but I stopped her. "We got this, Mom. Go on and get ready for work and by the time you get back the kitchen will be sparkling. All we need is a pinch and a twist, right, Mr. Gedrick?"

Mr. Gedrick nodded, but he was in work mode, so his expression didn't change.

"Come on, runt," Fergus said with a sigh. "Let's get this over with."

Mom looked relieved at the simple idea that her kids had been fed a good breakfast and she would have a little time alone to shower and get dressed. She looked lighter than she had in months. But then the phone rang. I was standing right next to where she'd left her phone sitting, and since I was in a very helping mood, I answered the call for Mom on speakerphone.

"Howdy," I said. "Darrow residence at your service."

"Hello? Elsa?" the person on the other end said. "It's me, Huxley."

"Oh, good morning, Mr. Harvold. It's early for you to call."

"Early? It's eight a.m. I've already jogged five miles and put in seven phone calls. Wait—eight phone calls, including this one."

"Well, that *is* a lot," Mom said. "What can I do for you, Mr. Harvold?"

"The deadline for the community arts center plans has been moved up a week. I hope that's not going to be a problem."

Mom snatched the phone from the table but

fumbled with the speakerphone button. "Uh . . . I don't know, Mr. Harvold. I was hoping for six more weeks. It's a very ambitious—"

"Wonderful, five more weeks it is then," Mr. Harvold butted in. "And I'd like to come by and see how it's going. Say tomorrow afternoon?"

"Oh, you don't want to drive all the way out here to the suburbs. It's coming along splendidly. Just need a pinch and a twist is all."

"A what and a what?"

"Never mind," she said. "Really, there's no need to come visit."

"I'll see you tomorrow then, say noon. Looking forward to it."

And then Huxley hung up on Mom.

"Mr. Harvold? Hello? Hello?" Mom said, but it was no use.

"Your boss sounds . . . demanding," Mr. Gedrick said as he toweled off a plate.

"You don't know the half of it. He's a real climber. I think he has plans to take over the company. Unfortunately, this community arts center is a big part of his big plan. Ugh."

"I know the type," Mr. Gedrick said. "Be careful, Ms. Darrow. Mr. Harvold may have plans that benefit him, not you."

"He's not the easiest boss in the world," Mom said.

"But it's me that's the problem. I just can't seem to get inspired lately."

Mr. Gedrick didn't say anything else. He went back to the dishes instead.

"You can do it, Mom!" I said. "We'll be done in here in a zip and a zap—then the whole day is yours to work work work."

Mom decided to skip the shower and just change her clothes. When she walked back to the kitchen a few minutes later, we were all standing in a line. The kitchen was cleaned to perfection, and the coffeepot had been moved to her table with a fresh cup.

"Everything all right?" Mr. Gedrick asked as he took off his apron and folded it many times. He folded and folded, and the apron got smaller and smaller. Then he placed it in the inside pocket of his green felt jacket.

"You gotta show me how you do that trick," Fergus said.

"It's not a trick," I said. "It's *magic*."

Fergus rolled his eyes.

Mom shook her head, confused by what she was seeing and wondering if she was still half-asleep. "You guys are getting really good at cleaning this kitchen."

"Eight hands are one hundred times faster than two, remember?" I said.

She took a deep breath and looked at her table full of empty paper. "Everybody out, I've got some serious work to do."

Fergus said he was going to Ernie's house early for the game so he could wake him up and make him play catch in his backyard. Amelia had locked herself in her room. So that left just me and Mr. Gedrick in the kitchen, staring at Mom.

"I'd like to see the garage," Mr. Gedrick said. "Who's joining me?"

"I will!" I shouted. Maybe now I could finally get some weight lifting in.

With the kitchen cleared and the leftovers put away, Mom sat down at her table and opened up her laptop. Mr. Gedrick was already in the garage, but I stayed in the opening of the door and quietly watched Mom. She stared and stared at the blank screen, but nothing happened. She tapped her pencil—tap tap tap—and placed it behind her ear. She got up and went to the refrigerator and opened the door.

"Maybe just one more waffle."

I quietly pulled the door to the garage shut and stood behind it. *Come on, Mom, you can do it. I know you can!*

THE PERFECT PLACE FOR A PROJECT
〜℮℮〜

Once I was in the garage, I went straight to the bench press and got into position. My hands barely reached the bar, and there were no weights on it.

"Hey, Mr. Gedrick, would you mind giving me a little help on this?" I asked.

But Mr. Gedrick was very busy looking around the garage, taking in its contents. We have a wall of power tools—drills and saws and sanders—and he seemed to like that.

"Those are my dad's tools," I said from the bench press. "He liked to build stuff."

Mr. Gedrick walked over and adjusted a saw that hung on the wall, tipping it slightly to the left. He took out his field guide and jotted down a few notes, then turned toward the largest thing in the space. I was disappointed that Mr. Gedrick didn't appear to have any interest in helping me lift the bar.

"It's an old Airstream," I said as I sat up on the bench. Our garage was big, three bays. The Airstream trailer took up most of one bay, the middle of the garage was empty, and the third bay was filled with the workbench, the wall of power tools, and the bench press, plus some other junk.

Mr. Gedrick took a long look at the Airstream. "I know what it is. A 1956 model, if I'm not mistaken."

"My dad was going to fix it up like a fort inside, but he never got around to it," I said. "So about this bench-press situation, I could really use a hand."

Mr. Gedrick walked right up to the trailer and touched the metal. It was round on top, not very big, all silver and shiny with a small door to go inside. The wheels seemed to be spinning in his head as he wrote down more notes in his field guide.

Then Mr. Gedrick turned to the giant globe and his dark eyebrows lowered. He scowled at the globe, like it didn't belong in the garage with the rest of the things.

"What do we have here?" he asked as he walked toward it.

"That's my dad's old globe. He used to show me all

kinds of stuff on there. It was like exploring without leaving the house."

"Interesting," Mr. Gedrick said. He spun the globe and watched it go, like he wished he could visit some of the places he saw.

"I found Swoghollow on there," I said. I wasn't sure if I should mention it, because it seemed like a secret sort of thing.

"Did you now?" Mr. Gedrick said, glancing at me. "That really is something."

"I know, right?" I ran to the globe and spent the next few minutes trying to locate Swoghollow, but I couldn't find it.

"I really did see it," I said. But had I? Maybe I had just *wanted* to see it.

"Swoghollow is hard to find," Mr. Gedrick said. "Even if you've found it once before."

"But I really did find it," I said. I got a feeling in the back of my throat and thought I might cry, which I really did not want to do.

"Are you feeling angry, Stanley?" Mr. Gedrick asked.

I spun the globe again and kept searching for Swoghollow. Something about the globe and the garage was really bothering me.

"You spent a lot of time here with Mr. Darrow, did you not?"

"We did like exploring this globe. It was one of my favorite things to do with him."

Mr. Gedrick knelt down next to me and put a hand on my shoulder. "It's okay to be angry sometimes. How about we try to channel that feeling into something useful."

"Like what?" I asked.

Mr. Gedrick glanced at the bench press then turned back to me.

"I don't know," I said as I stared at the bench press, too. "I think that bar might make me even more frustrated."

"How about we try anyway?" Mr. Gedrick asked.

I took a big breath and let it out. Then I went to the bench press and sat down.

"I can't do it, Mr. Gedrick. I'm too small."

"Nonsense. All you have to do is believe, and it will practically lift itself."

"I do believe. I believe that thing is trying to kill me."

Mr. Gedrick didn't say anything else. He stood quietly and waited, staring at the Airstream until I couldn't stand the silence anymore.

"Fine," I said as I lay down halfheartedly on the bench. "But you gotta back me up here. If this thing gets stuck on my chest, bail me out, okay?"

Mr. Gedrick didn't answer, and I felt struck by the wimpiness of my own arms.

I looked at each one. "It's just you and me, guys, let's do this."

I reached up and grabbed the bar. It slid off the cradles, descending onto my chest like an elephant.

"Ugh," I wheezed. "This thing is going to murder me."

As I stared at the ceiling, Mr. Gedrick's face came into view. He leaned over, staring at me. Mr. Gedrick took out his pointer and extended it. Then he tapped me on the head with it three times fast.

"Not helpful," I said as I struggled to breathe under the weight of the bar. I was thinking about sliding out from under it and landing on the hard floor. I felt even more frustrated and angry. Did Mr. Gedrick *want* me to fail?

"Close your eyes, Stanley," Mr. Gedrick said.

"Trouble breathing here," I complained.

"Close your eyes and listen to me carefully," Mr. Gedrick ordered in a soft but firm voice.

I didn't want to close my eyes. I wanted to lift the bar and throw it at the mailbox. I was mad at the bar, mad that my dad was gone, mad that my brother and sister didn't like me. Just plain mad. The bar felt like my whole life, everything weighing down on me, making me feel small and afraid. But I closed my eyes anyway. What else was I going to do?

"I want you to imagine something for me. Imagine

that there is no bar. Instead, you're holding a broomstick. The broom part is gone, it's just the stick in your hands. It hardly weighs anything at all. Light as a feather. Now I'm going to tap your forehead three more times, and you're going to lift that broom handle off your chest and put it back where it belongs."

I thought about the broom handle and how much it weighed. It was like a giant toothpick, and I was sure I could lift a giant toothpick.

I felt three taps on my forehead, and then I pushed as hard as I could. The bar lifted off my chest about three inches, then moved slowly back down again, like a balloon losing its air.

"I can't do it, Mr. Gedrick!" I yelled.

"You can!" Mr. Gedrick yelled back. He tapped my head three more times.

I pushed even harder this time. I pushed so hard I farted. It was a high, squeaky, waffle fart and it should have made me laugh and lose focus. But I kept at it. My noodle arms started to give out but I forced one more giant push.

"What's this contraption?" Mr. Gedrick asked.

Mr. Gedrick moved away, over by the big workbench, and I could hardly believe my one and only helper had left me. When I opened my eyes, I sat up and looked at Mr. Gedrick.

"Thanks a lot, pal," I said. "Here I am pinned like

a bug and you just leave me to get squished. Very nice."

But then I realized something. I wasn't lying down anymore. And the bar wasn't on my chest, it was sitting in its cradle, right where it belonged. I looked at the bar, blown away at what I had done.

"You were saying?" Mr. Gedrick said, looking down his pointed nose at me.

I started jumping up and down. "I did it! I finally lifted that stupid bar! I'm amazing!"

Mr. Gedrick smiled, but only for the flash of a moment. "Yes, Stanley. You are amazing. Don't forget it. Not ever."

I grinned from ear to ear. How had I done it? It had seemed so heavy before, an impossible thing to lift. But there it was.

"I was asking you about this contraption," Mr. Gedrick said, swishing his pointer to the right.

"That's a cage me and my dad built," I said. "Bob lives in there."

"Bob?"

"Yeah, he's a lizard. He was my dad's pet, but now we all take turns feeding him. Actually, I feed him mostly. Amelia and Fergus are too busy."

The cage was small but there were different places to hide, so Bob wasn't noticeable right away. There were four levels to the cage, and it was built of wood and wire with a small metal door. It looked like a scale model for a little house.

"You're good at building things," Mr. Gedrick said as he peered inside and got a look at Bob. They stared at each other, the guy and the lizard, for a long time.

"My dad did most of the work," I said, just to break the silence. "I helped a little."

The truth was, I'd always felt like the under-achiever in the family. Maybe it was because I was small or because I was the youngest. I couldn't draw or design stuff like my sister or Mom, and I wasn't great at sports like Fergus.

I walked over with a slouch in my step and unlatched the gate, then I took Bob out and showed him to Mr. Gedrick.

"He's a very thoughtful lizard," Mr. Gedrick said.

I had to agree. "You might be right. Bob's not much of a talker, that's for sure."

Mr. Gedrick eyeballed Bob. "How are the accom-modations, do they suit you? And the food, how's that? And are you being visited enough? Have you had any adventures lately?"

I watched as Bob's head turned to the left and he blinked twice. Then his tongue shot out and back in again.

"Very interesting," Mr. Gedrick said.

I looked up at Mr. Gedrick. "What did he say?"

"I think Bob is itching for a good adventure. But I've been wrong before."

I carefully put Bob back in the cage and latched the door shut.

"This might be the perfect place for a project of our own," Mr. Gedrick said, looking around the garage. He had a gleam in his green eyes. "A really *big* project."

Mr. Gedrick turned and stood in front of the wall of power tools.

"We need some plans," he said. "And for that, we're going to need your sister."

I wasn't too happy about getting Amelia involved. But I had to admit, plans are important on a big project. And Amelia was very good at drawing up plans.

"You're probably right," I said. "Should we go ask her?"

We agreed it was the right thing to do, and I started to leave. When I turned back, Mr. Gedrick was standing by Bob's cage leaning down like he was talking.

"Come on, Mr. Gedrick. We need plans if we're going to build something big."

Mr. Gedrick turned around and faced me. "How right you are. Lead the way."

A Disturbance in the Force

Our meeting with Amelia started out with a truck-load of ridiculous excuses about why she couldn't help us. There was absolutely positively no way she had time to make a plan for us.

Some of the excuses included:

"I am observing 'International Don't Leave Your Room Day,' and I take these things very seriously."

"I'm working on my bucket list. Your plan isn't on it."

"My palm reader advised against making any plans today."

And this zinger:

"There's a disturbance in the Force. And I never make plans when that happens."

I thought that last one was reasonable. I'd second-guess a big project if there was something sketchy with the Force, too.

But then Mr. Gedrick told Amelia what the plans were for, and the tide turned for us.

"That's actually a really nice idea," she said. She put the end of her pencil in her mouth and thought more about it.

"I'm going to need measurements, and right after that, *complete* alone time. *Total* silence. None of this racket in the middle of the night."

"Consider it done," Mr. Gedrick said.

Amelia thought a little more, and then pointed to the door like it was time for us to leave. "And I'll need some big sheets of paper. Also someone to bring me lunch. Knock on the door and leave it outside. Thanks."

I looked at Mr. Gedrick and we basically read each other's minds: *Mom has plenty of those big pieces of paper. We can distract her and pinch a couple of sheets.* We winked at each other.

"We have a deal," Mr. Gedrick said. "When can you deliver the goods?"

Amelia hesitated. She tapped the end of her pencil on her forehead several times. "Give me until tonight and I should have a beginning you can review."

"Hey, that's great!" I said. I was itching to get my hands on those power tools. "Did I mention that I lifted the whole bar all by myself? That thing weighs like a thousand pounds."

"That's great, Stanley," she said after a pause. I think she felt a little jealous of Mr. Gedrick helping me out. "And I'm sorry I didn't help you when you asked me to all those times. I'm sure Mr. Gedrick was there when you needed him."

"Not really," I said. "He sort of left me hanging. But I did it anyway!"

She looked up at Mr. Gedrick in his red tie and his green jacket and smiled a tiny bit.

This seemed to make Mr. Gedrick happy, and he hustled me down the hallway. He turned back to Amelia as her door was about to shut. "We'll leave you to your work and get that paper you need."

The door closed and Mr. Gedrick knelt down and put his face kind of close to mine. He had spearmint breath.

"You know, she doesn't really like being alone all the time. It's just become a habit she's fallen into since your dad hasn't been here."

"I miss her sometimes," I said. "It would be super nice to have her back."

In the living room, we came up with a plan to get several large pieces of paper from Mom's stash. I took off in one direction, and Mr. Gedrick in another. About a minute later the doorbell rang.

I was hiding around the side of the kitchen door and watched Mom. She didn't look up from her work. She stood there with a pencil in her mouth and another one in her hand, drawing out something on one of those big, fancy pieces of paper. The sheets were gigantic, about three feet by three feet, and I had to get at least two of them.

The doorbell rang again and Mom took the pencil out of her mouth. "Is someone going to get that? Anyone? Hello?"

The doorbell rang a third time and Mom finally went to see who it was. She walked past me as I lay flat against the wall. I tiptoed into the kitchen as Mom answered the door—it was Mr. Gedrick.

"Well, hello, Elsa," Mr. Gedrick said. "How's the work coming along? Splendidly, I hope."

"It's good," I heard Mom say as I approached her worktable. "I mean, actually, it's slow. Why are you ringing the doorbell?"

"Ah yes, the doorbell," Mr. Gedrick said. "I had a question about the lawn, and the lawn is out here. So naturally I rang."

"Of course you did. I'm right in the middle of this work, so can it wait until after dinner?"

I pulled up three sheets off the stack. Boy, they were really big. I had to hold my arms up to keep them from dragging on the kitchen floor.

"This won't take but a moment, a blip," Mr. Gedrick said. He put an arm toward Mom and I watched him guide her out onto the front porch. I quietly moved closer and hid behind the kitchen island as they talked.

"You see, I'd like to plant some flowers there, there, and there. And do some trimming on the lawn there, there, and there. And possibly work on those hedges there, there, and there. And I have some ideas about this big tree. Would that be all right with you?"

Mom didn't hesitate. The yard was a mess. Why not let him go to work on it? "Yes, yes, and yes. And also thank you. I didn't know you were also a gardener."

"I'll get Fergus to help me," Mr. Gedrick said. "We'll snip snap and chip chop and this will all look marvelous."

"Okay then," Mom said impatiently. "Is there anything else I can do for you, Mr. Gedrick?"

"No, no, that was all," he said. "I'll be in to make lunch shortly. Grilled cheese and tomato soup."

"Oh, that does sound good. Thank you, Mr. Gedrick. Thank you for everything."

"My pleasure. Oh, and did you hear Stanley lifted the bar off his chest? All by himself."

I felt a swell of pride and wished I could see Mom's face. That was when I dropped all three sheets and they fanned out on the kitchen floor like carpet squares.

"That's very good, Mr. Gedrick," Mom said from the porch. "He's a determined little boy."

"That he is."

I picked up the first two sheets, one in each hand, but I was having a hard time getting my fingers on to the last sheet since both hands were full. This was going to be tight.

"I'm going to go back to my work now," Mom said. She was heading for the door! "I'll look forward to seeing what becomes of the front yard."

I looked up and Mr. Gedrick was staring at me through the kitchen door. He could see the plan to get the paper was in big trouble. I was still standing in the kitchen and Mom was heading back!

"If I may, Ms. Darrow," he said. "Just one more thing. What's your opinion of yard gnomes?"

"Yard gnomes?"

"Yes, yard gnomes."

I finally got that third piece of paper by leaning down and grabbing it with my teeth. When I stood back up I nodded at Mr. Gedrick and ran down the hallway. The last thing I heard was Mom saying she thought yard gnomes were kind of silly, but if that's what Mr. Gedrick wanted, go for it.

We delivered the paper to Amelia's room, Mr. Gedrick made lunch, and the day crawled by with books and games and puzzles as we waited for the plans. We played one of my favorite games called Snorta! It's a game where you have to make a lot of animal sounds, which is something I'm really good at. Mr. Gedrick turned out to be a real master of the snort, the moo, and the bark, but the real kicker was his goose sound. The guy could honk like nobody's business.

"Is there a water fowl in the house?" Mom yelled from the kitchen.

"Nope, just us pigs and cows and dogs," I yelled back.

Mr. Gedrick made the honking sound again and I thought it was so hilarious I rolled around on the floor and knocked a lamp off the table. Good thing Mr. Gedrick was fast at catching falling lamps or Mom would have had a fit.

We waited and waited and waited. Unfortunately for us, it was going to take a lot more than a few rounds of Snorta! to get our plans from Amelia.

Someplace New

Amelia stalled over and over and eventually stopped answering our knocks at her door. I even tried bribing her with candy and quarters, but she wouldn't take the bait. It became clear that the plans wouldn't be ready for at least a couple of days. Fergus and Mom were nodding off by nine thirty p.m., but I was full of energy. I couldn't sleep as my mind raced about using power tools and building something cool. Mr. Gedrick and I were in the kitchen, where I was eating a bowl of cereal and he was making notes in his field guide. It looked like he was making plans of his own, but he wouldn't tell me what they were no matter how many times I asked him.

"When she gets here, I'd like you to turn in for the night," Mr. Gedrick said. "Can you do that for me?"

"When who gets here?" I asked through the crunching of my cereal.

Mr. Gedrick's eyebrow went up and he seemed to be listening for something quiet and faraway.

"She's on her way," he said. "Time for you to get going. Chop-chop."

A few seconds later, Amelia arrived in the kitchen. She was startled to find me and Mr. Gedrick sitting at the table.

"Whoa, neat trick, Mr. G.," I said.

"You scared me," Amelia said as she sat down next to us.

Mr. Gedrick closed his field guide and put it back in his jacket pocket. He raised an eyebrow at me.

"Oh right," I said, then I fake yawned. "Boy, I'm pooped. I guess I'll go to bed now."

I set my bowl in the sink and fake yawned again, even louder this time. But when I got into the living room, I stopped. No way was I going to miss an important update about the plans. I crept closer and stayed quiet as a mouse.

"Don't you ever sleep?" Amelia asked.

"I sleep when the work is finished, and I had a feeling it wasn't quite done yet."

"What's that supposed to mean?"

Mr. Gedrick paused, then he asked the question I was most curious about. "How's the plan coming along?"

Another pause, and then Amelia said, "I don't work well under pressure."

"I understand."

There was another space of silence. Then Amelia said, "All this blank paper, and all those wadded-up pieces in the garbage can. I don't know what's wrong with her."

"It appears you're not the only one who doesn't work well under pressure."

"What about you?" Amelia asked. I peeked around the corner and saw her staring up at the strange man with the green jacket and the red tie. "Why do you care about our family? What's in it for you?"

Mr. Gedrick looked at Amelia for a long moment and then shook his head. He wasn't going to talk about that, not now anyway.

"She's not going to be disappointed in you," Mr. Gedrick said. "She's too busy being disappointed in herself."

Amelia touched the paper. She let her fingers slide along the slick surface. "She's really good at this stuff. I don't know why she's struggling so much."

"Sometimes inspiration comes on its own schedule," Mr. Gedrick said. "And sometimes it wants to come in, but it can't find the doorway."

"What do you mean?" Amelia asked, eyes glued to Mr. Gedrick. It was like she hoped he had answers she couldn't find on her own.

"Sometimes, when something very difficult happens, it's impossible to find the way back to where you once were," Mr. Gedrick said. "There's a reason for that."

"What's the reason?" Amelia asked.

Mr. Gedrick leaned forward and put his elbows on the table. He folded his hands.

"We're not supposed to go back to where we were. There's someplace new, out there, waiting for us. We only have to go and find it. And when we do, then the inspiration will find us once again."

I started to feel like I was going to cry, because I knew exactly how Amelia felt when Mr. Gedrick said those things. I knew because I felt that way, too. She couldn't go back—neither could I. There's no *there* there. Our dad was gone.

"You're asking me to forget about my dad, to leave him behind."

Mr. Gedrick stood up and looked at his watch. "Time goes forward, Amelia. It doesn't stand still or move in reverse. Mr. Darrow would have wanted you to move on. He would want you to be happy again."

"You didn't even know my dad. You don't know what you're talking about."

Mr. Gedrick's face softened and he nodded. "Things aren't always as they seem at first glance."

"What's that supposed to mean?"

Whatever lesson Mr. Gedrick was trying to teach my sister wasn't working.

"She's not making much progress," Amelia said, staring back at the blank paper and holding back tears.

"Not true," Mr. Gedrick said. "Look how full the garbage can is? All the ideas on the way to the great idea are in there. She's closer than she thinks she is."

"The ideas on the way to the great idea. Sounds like a lot of work."

"That it is," Mr. Gedrick agreed.

Amelia said good night and that was my cue to run like the wind. She'd left her door open and I looked inside as I went past. She had crumpled up all the papers I'd brought her. They were around the room like pieces of dirty laundry.

I cut across the hall and slipped into my room before Amelia showed up. A minute later I was in bed listening to Fergus snore.

"You can find your way again," I said, thinking of my sister. "You can do this. Also we need those plans or I don't get to use the power tools, and that would be a huge bummer."

Buckminster Fuller

The next morning I heard a light tapping on my door and looked over at the clock.

It was six a.m.

The soft knock came again, and this time the door opened a crack and Mr. Gedrick's eyeball peered inside.

"Meet me at Fred in two minutes," he whispered. "And keep quiet on our little trip. This isn't for you, it's for her." Then the door shut again.

Yes! I loved Fred, so I hoped this meant we were going for another wild ride around the neighborhood. I didn't bother to change out of my pajamas. When I got out into the hallway, Mr. Gedrick was tapping on Amelia's door.

"Why am I awake?" I heard her murmur unhappily.

"Come along," Mr. Gedrick said. "I have something to show you."

"Come back in three hours," Amelia said.

"I'm quite sure we need to go now," Mr. Gedrick said. "In a few hours, it will be open."

This, like so many things Mr. Gedrick said and did, made absolutely no sense.

"Don't ask about the plan," Amelia said. "It's not ready yet."

"I know," Mr. Gedrick said. "It will be ready when it's ready. That's the only time things *are* ready."

"When they're ready," Amelia parroted.

"Off we go then," Mr. Gedrick said, and I ran to the front door before Amelia could see me. I wanted it to be a surprise. I jumped right into Fred's sidecar and watched as they arrived on the front porch.

"If you're taking me outside to pick weeds, I'd like to remind you that child labor is illegal in the United States."

Mr. Gedrick didn't respond as he walked toward Fred.

"A convertible," Amelia said, brightening. "Now we're talking."

"Hey there, guys!" I said, waving from the sidecar.

"Where does he get the energy?" Amelia

wondered aloud as she walked down to the driveway, rubbing the sleep out of her eyes.

Mr. Gedrick was in the driver's seat seconds later, wrapping the old-style seat belt around his waist. He took the driving goggles out of the glove box, pulled them over his head, and turned to his companion.

"Buckle up," he said, petting the dashboard. "Fred isn't too happy to be up early either. This is likely to be a bumpy ride."

"Yeah, buckle up," I said, crouching down in my little compartment like a race car driver.

"Who's Fred?" Amelia asked.

The second he heard the click of Amelia's seat belt, Mr. Gedrick backed up with ferocious speed, slammed the gearshift forward, and blasted down the empty street.

"You weren't kidding about the seat belt!" Amelia shouted.

"Awesome, right?!" I added.

We sped out of the neighborhood onto a four-lane road and then onto the freeway. The wind was whipping my hair all over the place and I wished I'd brought my baseball cap.

"Were you a race car driver in a previous life?" Amelia yelled.

"Only in my dreams," Mr. Gedrick said, slamming his foot down on the gas and whooshing past a semi.

At the speed we were going, it didn't take long to reach our destination, which turned out to be the Art Institute of Chicago. It's a big stone building with two green lions standing in front, apparently guarding the place. Mr. Gedrick parked in the shadow of the lions and took his goggles off. He ran his hands along his hair, which was standing on end, and when he was done, he looked as perfectly put together as ever. Amelia, on the other hand, looked like she'd just gone through a cycle in a washing machine.

"You look nuts!" I said.

"Join the club, little brother. It looks like you just stuck a fork in a light socket."

"Everyone still in one piece?" Mr. Gedrick asked.

"Barely," Amelia said, but she looked as happy as I'd seen her in a long time. "What are we doing here? They're not even open."

"Precisely," Mr. Gedrick said.

He exited the car and we followed, chasing him down as he took two stone steps at a time to the entrance.

"Wait for me!" Amelia said. "Also, we can't go in there. Like I said, they're not open. It was a nice ride all the same."

Mr. Gedrick ignored her until he reached the front door. He rapped on it three times with his knuckles.

Amelia caught up and stood next to Mr. Gedrick.

"I told you already. We can't get in there."

Just about that time a man appeared on the other side of the glass door. He spied Mr. Gedrick, and turned a key in the lock.

Mr. Gedrick looked down at Amelia with one of his half smiles. "You were saying?"

He held the door open for me and Amelia, and I thought about what he had said to me back at home. *This isn't for you, it's for her.* I made a mental note to stay quiet.

"Thank you, Walter," Mr. Gedrick said. "Would you mind keeping an eye on Fred? He's right there, by the lion."

"Of course, Mr. Gedrick," the man said. "You have an hour. Take your time."

"Brilliant," Mr. Gedrick said as he whisked Amelia inside the grand building. I let myself fall a little behind so they could have their privacy.

"Are we going to jail for this?" Amelia asked nervously. I had never been in a building that wasn't open and neither had she, let alone a famous museum. "Because if we are, I should have brought actual shoes. Jail in floppy slippers sounds like a terrible idea."

"Follow me," Mr. Gedrick said. "The items I'd like to show you are thisaway."

We rushed past many paintings and sculptures,

but Mr. Gedrick didn't stop in front of any of them. Amelia kept asking him questions as she passed more and more things: *Is this what you want me to see? Or this? Or that?* But they kept on going, deeper into the museum. Amelia's floppy slippers slapped on the bottoms of her feet, echoing down the long, empty corridors.

We came to a wide door that was closed, and finally, Mr. Gedrick stopped. He knelt down next to Amelia so she could look into his eyes.

"Behind this door lies inspiration," Mr. Gedrick said, glancing at his watch. "You have fifty-one minutes. Make the most of them."

Now Amelia was excited. No one had ever brought her to a door and said words like that. I felt butterflies in my stomach.

"Do you know, my dad used to bring me here sometimes," she said, inching forward and putting her hand on the door handle. "The boys didn't like it so much, but I did, so he would take only me."

"That's true," I said. "I'm not a big art buff. But this is still cool."

"I suspect those are very good memories," Mr. Gedrick said to Amelia. "Very good indeed."

Amelia nodded. "I always brought a drawing pad with me, and he brought one, too. His drawings were awful, stick figures and square houses. But he always drew right along with me. I liked that about him. He would do things he wasn't any good at, just because I didn't want to do them alone."

"You learned something from those times," Mr. Gedrick said. "You're observant, Amelia."

Amelia smiled at Mr. Gedrick and pulled the heavy door open. I scurried through behind both of them before it shut in my face.

Inside was a room filled with strange, round objects. On the wall leading in there was a name that was even stranger.

"Who is Buckminster Fuller?" Amelia asked. "And why does he have such a goofy name?"

Mr. Gedrick waved his hand across the room. "Mr. Fuller made all of these things, only they were much bigger when he made them. These are only models. He was an architect, like your mother. Like you."

"Oh, I'm not an architect. I just draw things for fun."

But even as she said it I could tell she wished and wished that she *was* an architect. She had always loved the idea of designing hotels, libraries, and skyscrapers.

"We shall see about that," Mr. Gedrick said.

He took her to the first of many large pedestals with one of the round objects on top.

Amelia was mesmerized by the weirdness of it. "This is a building?"

"That it is," Mr. Gedrick answered. "A very famous one. He designed it for the 1967 World Expo. It was large—big enough to put hundreds of people inside."

The smaller version looked like something that belonged on Mars or at Disneyland. It was round and white. I could tell Amelia loved it.

"And is this a house?" Amelia asked, racing over to another pedestal. There was only half a dome on this one, cut down the middle so we could see inside.

"Precisely," Mr. Gedrick said, "it's a round house."

"It looks like a barn but the middle is a big bubble shaped like a golf ball," I said.

Mr. Gedrick eyeballed me—*zip it, Stanley*—and I zipped it. I mean I actually did. I ran my fingers across my lips and zipped my mouth shut. Then I threw away the key.

Amelia looked up at Mr. Gedrick. "I love Buckminster Fuller."

"I thought you might."

"Did you bring any paper? And a pencil?" Amelia asked.

Mr. Gedrick had an extra field guide, and he took it out of his green felt jacket, handing it to Amelia. There was already a pencil tucked inside, with a nice sharp point.

"*Architecture Field Guide*," Amelia said, reading the cover. "Is this for me?"

Mr. Gedrick nodded, and then he looked at his watch again. "Forty-six more minutes. Better make haste."

After that, Mr. Gedrick answered a lot of questions as Amelia went from dome to dome, making notes and small drawings in the field guide. Some of the domes were cut in half so she could see inside, where she found odd-looking desks and tables and rooms. She drew more and more, and then she came to a very large circular dome sitting on the floor.

"Can I go inside?" she asked, because there was an open entryway. I wanted to go in there in the worst way, but it was Amelia's day, so I pretended my shoes were glued to the floor. It's a good thing I had all the imaginary glue and zippers or I'd have been freaking out left and right.

"I think Mr. Fuller and Mr. Darrow would want you to go inside," Mr. Gedrick said. "No doubt about it."

Somehow I felt like she might find Dad inside, waiting for her with a big smile on his face. He would say things like *Don't you just love how nutty this house is?* or *You could make one of these in the backyard, I'm sure of it.* I could tell that she felt Dad all around—I felt it, too—even if he wasn't there. I went to the door and watched her as she looked at the curved glass and yellow furniture and soft cushions. She moved around the room, taking it all in.

"Mr. Gedrick." A voice came from the door. It was Walter, who had let us in. "Just a few more minutes."

"Of course, thank you, Walter," Mr. Gedrick said.

Amelia didn't want to go yet—this place was too exciting. But I could tell she also wanted to leave, because she was feeling inspired to draw. Perfect for me! This meant we were one step closer to getting ahold of those plans.

A half hour later when we pulled into the driveway, Amelia turned to Mr. Gedrick. She had been drawing and drawing all the way, hardly looking up as Mr. Gedrick took things a little slower. He knew it was hard to draw in a speeding car.

"Fred doesn't often enjoy a slow drive," Mr. Gedrick explained. "But he knew you were working on something important. Sometimes, slow is best. Even for a speed demon."

"I hope you take your own advice," Amelia offered. "Good plans take time, they can't be rushed."

"You should tell that to your mother. She's awfully hard on herself."

Amelia nodded quietly as she looked at the notes and drawings she'd done.

"Thank you for taking me there."

Amelia hesitated for a second and then said one more thing. "I think I'm ready to make your plans."

"Wonderful," Mr. Gedrick said. "I am so pleased."

She leaned across the seat and gave Mr. Gedrick a hug, then ran to the front door and disappeared inside.

"Can I unzip my lip now?" I asked.

"Not quite yet."

I got out of the sidecar and waited.

Mr. Gedrick took out his field guide to the Darrows and jotted down a few quick notes.

"It's all connected," he said.

"What is?"

"Time, magic, grief, renewal."

I really wanted to unzip my mouth and say something, but I could tell Mr. Gedrick was in one of his thinking moods so I didn't.

Then we wandered into the house and got to talking about plans and power tools and breakfast.

Bob Takes a Hike

I went to my room to tell Fergus all about the adventure I'd just been on. Fergus was only half-awake, and he kept telling me to stop talking or get out. We started to argue, because I had already been quiet for like two hours and I *really* wanted to talk. But then there was a new, fantastic smell coming from the kitchen and Fergus couldn't keep his eyes closed anymore.

"He has *got* to stop working in the kitchen so early in the morning," Fergus said. He sat up and grumbled some more, then his stomach rumbled. "Come on, little man. Let's go see what's cooking."

It turned out to be something Mr. Gedrick called

monkey bread. It was soft and chewy and covered in some kind of caramel sauce. It felt like waking up in a French bakery.

We polished off the whole thing in ten minutes flat, and then we all went to the garage while Mom got ready for her meeting with Huxley Harvold. Amelia had a rolled-up tube of paper in one hand, and she stared nervously at the concrete floor.

"I've got baseball practice in an hour," Fergus said. He didn't want to be stuck in the garage any longer than he had to be. "What's this all about?"

"I told you already," I said. "It's a *plan*. Something we can work on together. And we get to use Dad's power tools!"

"You mean *I* get to use the power tools," Fergus corrected. "You can use the hammer as long as you don't hit your thumb with it."

I looked at Mr. Gedrick for support, but he wouldn't back me up.

"Stanley!" Fergus yelled. He had walked over to Bob's cage to say hi to the lizard.

"I'm standing right here," I said. "You don't have to yell."

But Fergus was mad when he turned toward everyone else. "You left Bob's cage open, dope. Now he's gone!"

I ran to the cage and tried to get my whole head inside the door, but my head was too big. I looked through all the openings and checked all the spots where Bob liked to sit.

"But that can't be," I said, my eyes darting all over the garage. "I'm sure I closed it."

"You fed him last," Fergus said. "That was Dad's pet. I can't believe this."

"You never spent time with him anyway," I said, my lower lip quivering. "Bob disappeared for you a long time ago."

Fergus stomped out of the garage, shaking his head. He didn't exactly love Bob and hadn't ever had much to do with him, but he was still mad our little lizard had escaped.

"Why'd Dad have to leave the dumb thing behind anyway?" Fergus said, his voice trailing back into the garage.

"Wait, Fergus," I said. "We need your help on the project. Don't go!"

But he was gone.

Amelia gripped the tube of paper she held on to—the plans!—and shook her head. She was barely holding it together. "Nice going, Stanley."

"It was an accident," I said. "Bob will come back. I know he will."

"I hope you're right," Amelia said, but I could tell she wasn't so sure. "One more part of Dad we can never get back again."

She walked out of the garage. Amelia was gone, and the plans went with her.

"This is a disaster," I said, and my eyes got blurry. I went back to the cage just to be sure Bob was really gone. "I ruined everything."

Mr. Gedrick knelt down close and put a hand on my back. "It might have been me who left the cage open. Or someone else. Or maybe Bob just got very tired of being in there and wanted to go on an adventure. Lizards are like that. They like to roam once in a while."

"They both hate me," I said. "They never want to play with me and they think I'm dumb. This just makes it worse."

"They don't hate you," Mr. Gedrick said. "They're just lost. But we're going to help them find their way again, together. Will you do that with me?"

I wiped my nose on the back of my hand and looked right into Mr. Gedrick's face. I could see he really cared. And I saw something else I'd seen before. He had that thoughtful, sad look. "I miss my dad so much. It hurts all over. And it's even worse because they ignore me. It's like I don't exist."

"I know, Stanley. I know," Mr. Gedrick said. He

hugged me and I felt the soft green of the jacket on my cheek.

Mr. Gedrick pulled back and held me by my shoulders. "Just because you're the smallest doesn't mean you can't do big things."

My eyes went wide. I couldn't believe the words I'd just heard.

"Hey! My dad was always telling me that."

"Really?" Mr. Gedrick asked.

"I remember the last time he said it. We were playing basketball in the driveway and I wished and wished that I could dunk the ball, but I was way too small. He told me the same thing—*just because you're the smallest doesn't mean you can't do big things*—then he lifted me up and I dunked the heck out of that ball. The backboard shook and everything. Fergus even saw me do it."

"Well, there you go," Mr. Gedrick said. "You *can* do big things, just as I suspected."

I looked at the floor and then at Bob's empty cage.

"Are you magic, Mr. Gedrick?" I asked. "How else would you know all about my dad?"

Mr. Gedrick smiled thoughtfully. "Magic is difficult to explain, Stanley. But the best kind is always for a good purpose. Let's search the garage. Bob has to be here somewhere."

We searched and searched, but didn't find Bob.

"Hey, look," I said as I crouched down next to the wall of hanging tools. "The door to the crawl space is open. That's weird."

The crawl space is under the house, and the opening isn't very big. It's built into the floor, only a couple of feet square.

"It's dark down there," I said.

"There's little doubt," Mr. Gedrick said, staring at the crawl space door. "Bob went in there. It's the perfect place for a lizard."

"But . . . ," I said. I wrung my hands and looked up at Mr. Gedrick. "Why would he do that? I'd *never* go down there."

"Are you sure about that? What if your friend was alone and lost; wouldn't you go looking for him?"

I didn't want to answer that question, so I stared at the floor some more. "I still don't think I'd go down there. I'm too afraid to do that."

"Oh, but you're the only one who can crawl around there quickly and efficiently," Mr. Gedrick said, his face lighting up with excitement. "Imagine how fast you'll find Bob if you only have the courage to try."

I paced back and forth. I thought about finding Bob and how surprised Fergus and Amelia would be. I took a couple of deep breaths and glanced at the bench press.

"You didn't think you could do that," Mr. Gedrick

said, eyeing the bench as well. "But you did."

I went to the wall of tools and grabbed a flashlight. I turned it on to make sure it was working, and then I went over to the crawl space and pointed the light inside. I put the flashlight in my back pocket and felt how heavy it was.

"I can't believe I'm doing this," I said. I walked back and forth some more, shaking my head. And then I cracked my knuckles like a prizefighter. "Bob, I'm on my way! Don't worry!"

I took the flashlight out and jumped down into the hole, then I started crawling in the darkness, the light dancing in front of my eyes.

Under and Around the House

There were cobwebs everywhere and I kept batting them away with my hand. Every few feet I yelled back to Mr. Gedrick and waited for a reply, and every time the voice I heard coming back was a little farther away. I could still see the light coming in from the garage, but it was like a night-light, far away.

"Bob, if you're down here, I could really use a little company," I said. I felt my hands shaking and almost dropped the flashlight. The ceiling overhead was low, so I had to crawl on my hands and knees. The cold dirt made me think about cemeteries and headstones.

"I can't do this," I said. "Mr. Gedrick! I'm coming back!"

I turned around awkwardly and started for the light coming out of the garage, but a couple of seconds later I wasn't so sure. I thought about Bob, stuck under the house with no crickets and no friends. So I turned around again and started crawling.

"I'm not going to let you die down here alone, Bob. Don't worry. I'm coming for you."

A big, hairy spider eyed me from a cobweb and I lurched upward, banging my head on a beam.

"Come on, house, whose side are you on here?" I said as I rubbed my head.

I took a wide turn around the spider, then crawled past a concrete block and farther into the darkness. It felt like I was a million miles from anyone else, all alone at the bottom of the world.

I started thinking about my dad, trying to keep my mind away from spiders and headstones and stuff like that. I remembered once when we were bowling at a birthday party, and I could hardly hold the ball even with two hands. I wanted a strike so bad, but when I threw the ball down the lane, it landed in the gutter. I turned around and looked at my dad, expecting him to be all disappointment. But he made me feel better.

I wished and wished that I could find Bob. I thought I heard something moving up ahead, and stopped in my tracks.

"That you, Bob?" I asked.

The sound moved to my left and I pointed the flashlight toward it. Then I screamed.

Two eyes were staring back at me, and they were way bigger than lizard eyes.

"Heeeeeeelp!" I yelled, but no one could hear me all the way under the house.

I heard the creature moving behind me and a shiver ran up my spine. I spun around, pointing the flashlight.

"Back, you beast! Back!" I yelled.

It was a possum. I am not a fan of possums. They freak me out. It was about ten feet away, but when I yelled at it, the possum wobbled away out of the light.

"Oh man, this is crazy. I'm going to have a heart attack."

I pointed the flashlight in every direction, searching for rats or more possums or possibly a wolf. My nerves were shot, my hands were shaking, and I was pouring sweat.

"I don't think I'm going to be able to save you, Bob. I'm sorry. I just can't stay down here anymore."

I went to turn around, defeated, and my flashlight landed on something in the corner under the house. It was the farthest corner from the crawl space door.

"Bob? Is that you?" I asked.

There were two little dots that looked like they might be eyes glowing in the dark.

"Or are you a huge rat that's going to bite into my arm and suck all my blood?"

I looked toward the exit one more time. I really wanted to leave, but it was only a little farther to make sure Bob wasn't waiting for me.

"You better be Bob or I'm going to punch you in the nose," I said. I imagined what it would feel like to punch a giant rat in the nose. I imagined the rat with boxing gloves, both of us in a ring taking jabs at each other. And by the time I imagined knocking the rodent out with a monster uppercut, I was at the farthest corner of the house.

"Bob!" I yelled. Bob looked bored to death, like he was about to take a nap.

"Hey, what are you doing all the way down here?" I asked. Bob squinted into the light and blinked.

I crawled forward until I was right next to Bob. I was feeling much better now that I wasn't alone. "There's a lot of weird stuff down here, huh? I saw a possum as big as a truck back there, scared the pants off me. Hey, what is that?"

Bob was sitting in the middle of a coiled-up rope. But it was no ordinary rope. This one was leather, like an Indiana Jones whip.

"Cool," I said. "You're a good little adventurer. I'm glad you're here. I was getting freaked out all by myself."

I only have two hands, and I sure wasn't going to put the flashlight down, so I picked up the strange leather rope and hung it around my neck. "Come on, Bob. Let's get the heck out of here."

I picked up Bob and crawled toward the tiny square of light from the garage. The way back was less scary than the way inside had been. In fact, I wasn't scared at all. I'd found my little buddy—and bonus—I'd found a treasure, too. When I popped my head back out into the garage, Mr. Gedrick was standing right there.

"One went in, but two came out," Mr. Gedrick said. "Well done, Stanley Darrow. Well done!"

"Thanks, Mr. Gedrick. You should have been there! I almost got eaten by a giant possum! And a hairy spider. And I got into a boxing match with a rat. And check out this cool rope thing I found."

I set the flashlight down and held out the rope. Mr. Gedrick seemed really curious about it. "Interesting. You found this under the house?"

"Actually, Bob found it under the house, then I found Bob," I said.

"What a clever lizard you have there," Mr. Gedrick said. He looked at the leather rope more carefully. "A very curious rope. I wonder what it could be for?"

"I have no idea," I said as Mr. Gedrick gave it back. "Maybe it belonged to the person who used to own the house."

"Or maybe someone hid it down there, for safe-keeping," Mr. Gedrick wondered. "Either way, you must take good care of it. Who knows what important use it might have?"

Mr. Gedrick's eyes twinkled and he got that small half smile on his face again, like magic was in the air.

"I'll take super good care of it," I said. "You can count on me."

"I know I can," Mr. Gedrick said. He looked at Bob's cage. "How about you and I build a bigger, better cage for Bob? Something magnificent. A place he'll never want to leave. It would be a good warm-up for the big plan Amelia just walked away with."

"Hey, that's a great idea!" I said. "Can I cut the wood?"

Mr. Gedrick didn't answer. He took out his pointer and extended it. Then he folded it very quickly many times and it ended up looking like a coat hanger. He took off his green felt jacket and hung it up, then he rolled up his sleeves.

"That pointer of yours is pretty neat," I said. "Want to trade it for my super cool rope?"

"Not on your life," Mr. Gedrick said. "Now let's get to work, shall we?"

"Yes, we shall!" I shouted. I put Bob back into the old cage and set the leather rope on the floor in the corner.

Mr. Gedrick stopped short and sniffed the air.

"You smell a possum?" I asked as I sniffed the air, too. "I'm not getting anything."

"Do me a favor, will you, Stanley?"

"Sure thing."

"Go around the front of the house. I think Mr. Harvold has arrived to see your mother. You're good at staying hidden—another bonus of being small, you see—and I'd like to make sure he doesn't put too much pressure on her."

I saluted Mr. Gedrick.

"Yes, sir!" I said.

I love playing spy games, so I was excited about this assignment.

"Don't start cutting stuff up until I get back," I said.

"No problem."

"Promise?"

"Yes, Stanley. I promise."

And with that, I went out the side garage door and worked my way toward the front of the house using my sneakiest spy skills.

Huxley Harvold

On my way to the front of the house I peeked into the kitchen window and saw Mom pacing back and forth. She was stress-eating from a bag of M&M's.

I heard a car door shut in the driveway, and continued on to the edge of the house. When I looked around the corner, Huxley Harvold was walking up to the front door.

I'd met Huxley before at Mom's old office. He's shaped like a pear, with a big gut and stumpy legs like an old football player. He's about halfway to bald, so he's got this long forehead that shines like a golf ball.

Huxley stood on the front porch and looked at our

lawn. There were weeds everywhere and it hadn't been mowed for weeks. It was so bad I almost felt embarrassed. Huxley shook his head and looked concerned.

"What a dope," I said, moving a little closer and hiding behind a big bush.

Mom had told me all about the Chicago Community Arts Center and how important it was. It was a showpiece, and the whole city was watching. If she couldn't deliver a bang-up plan on time, it would mean more than just serious egg on her face. Mom kept talking about the guy who ran the firm now, Mr. Jivins, and how she thought Huxley wants to push him out. I think Mom felt like she was being used in all this, and the project she was working on was some sort of chess piece.

Huxley ran his hands along the sleeves of his expensive suit jacket and adjusted his designer glasses. He rang the doorbell and seemed to brace himself for a difficult encounter.

And waited.

And waited.

I could hear the sound of power tools from the garage, so Huxley could hear it, too.

"Dang it, Mr. G., you were supposed to wait for me!" I whispered, almost too loudly. I wanted to run back to the garage and see what was going on, but

I'd been given a mission. And a spy never leaves a mission half done.

Just then, Mom opened the front door.

"Mr. Harvold," Mom said as she waved him into the house. "I'm sorry to keep you standing there. Won't you please come in?"

"I'd be delighted," Huxley said with a fake smile pasted on his face.

I skedaddled up the walkway and onto the front porch, then I turned the knob on the door super slowly. I opened the door just a pinch. They were still standing in the living room so I couldn't go in yet.

"The inside of your house is much nicer than I expected," Huxley said. "The outside threw me off. You really need a gardener, don't you think?"

Mom tried to ignore the comment while she ushered Huxley into the kitchen. I slipped through the door with the skill of a superspy and crawled along the floor behind the couch. All the crawling around under the house had given me plenty of practice.

"I've just made some coffee," Mom said a little too excitedly. "Would you like some?"

"I'm on a tight schedule and can't stay long," Huxley answered. "And I'm dying to see the plans!"

"Right, the plans," Mom said. She wiped her sweaty palms on her blouse and walked over to her worktable. That was my cue to move in close, right next to the doorway leading into the kitchen.

"Welcome to my office," Mom said. "Not a lot of privacy. On the upside, I can get to the refrigerator in three seconds flat."

She laughed awkwardly, and Huxley smiled and nodded like he really didn't care whether she ate all day or not at all. "Quite a lot of racket going on in the garage. That must be distracting for you."

"Oh no, not distracting," Mom said. "I like a lot of noise when I'm working. Keeps me focused."

Huxley looked sideways at Mom. "I see. How about we take a look at those plans?"

The sound of a power saw firing up in the garage made Mom jump. She held up a finger. "If you could excuse me for just one second. I'll get them to keep it down."

All I could think about was all the sawing I wasn't doing. It was driving me bananas.

"Guys, please," Mom yelled through the garage doorway. "Keep it down out here. I've got work to do. Lots of work. And I have a visitor."

Mom seemed to hope Mr. Gedrick would get the hint—*my boss is here!* She closed the door and turned back to the kitchen to find Huxley going through her things. He looked up at her with eyebrows raised. His glasses had slid down on his round nose.

"Is there something else you'd like to show me?" he asked. "Or is this all you have?"

The sound of a hammer pounding in the garage interrupted the silence between Mom and Huxley She pulled the door open again. "Guys!"

All the noise from the garage stopped in an instant. I wanted to yell *Thanks, Mom!* Anything that slowed Mr. Gedrick down was fine by me until I could get back in there.

"I have some things," Mom said, walking back to the table. She unrolled a tube of paper and laid it out for Huxley to see. "Nothing too detailed."

Huxley began flipping through the new stack of pages, looking more optimistic. "Oh, this is good. I like this one. And this one shows some promise."

Mom watched as Huxley looked more carefully at the designs. I could tell Mom's heart was sinking by the look on her face. I don't think any of it was what she wanted to do for the arts center. If it was, she would have showed it to him when he walked in. But Huxley was her boss, so what could she do?

"You have a long way to go," Huxley said. "But I like where this is heading. Maybe you should return to the office and finish the work there. The deadline is approaching and you can be more focused at work, don't you think?"

The hammering started up again in the garage.

"I'm sure I can work here and finish on time," Mom said. "It won't be a problem."

"The difference between a successful person and others is not a lack of strength or knowledge," Huxley said, looking gravely at Mom. "But rather a lack of will."

Mom nodded and smiled awkwardly, because as usual Huxley's advice made no sense.

"Now I must be going," Huxley said. "Don't let me down, Elsa. The whole firm is counting on you. We're expecting something big and bold and amazing. You can do that, right?"

"Oh yes, sir, I can do it. You don't need to worry about me."

"I'll let myself out," Huxley said as the sound of a saw got into full swing again. He smiled uncomfortably at Mom. I crawled to the door in record time, slipped out, and hightailed it for the garage.

Bob's New Habitat

"Mom, come see what we built!" I yelled as I opened the door that connected the garage to the kitchen. A few hours had passed since Huxley's visit, and I'd told Mr. Gedrick everything I'd seen. He'd said "I see" and "fascinating" a lot, but then he seemed to lose interest.

"What's for dinner?" Fergus asked as he breezed into the kitchen wearing his baseball clothes.

Mom put her pencil behind her ear but didn't get up. "Hello to you, too."

"Is this going to be another one of those make-my-own-dinner days?" Fergus asked impatiently. "I thought having a butler was going to include grub."

"Mr. Gedrick's not a butler," I said. "He's our nanny. And besides, he's been helping me work on something in the garage all day. It's cool, want to see?"

"What I want to see is a sandwich, some chips, and a Coke," Fergus complained.

I gave up on Fergus and ran down the hall. When I opened Amelia's door without even asking her, she chased me back into the living room.

"Come on, guys, you've got to see this," I said.

"Who gave Stanley sugar?" Amelia asked.

"Wasn't me, I was out kicking butt on the baseball field," Fergus said. He guzzled down half a can of soda.

"If baseball didn't exist, you'd be a formless blob of cells with no purpose in life," Amelia said.

Fergus burped then returned fire from the couch. "Sounds like you're speaking from experience, blob face."

Amelia stared daggers at Fergus's face and clenched her pencil like she wanted to stab it into his arm.

"Everyone stop talking," Mom said, and she looked at me. "I'd love to see what you've been building out there. We all would. Wouldn't we?"

She glared at Fergus and Amelia, and everyone followed me into the garage. Mr. Gedrick had his green felt jacket back on and he was wiping sawdust off his shiny shoes. When he stood up, everyone was together next to the workbench.

"You guys built that?" Amelia asked.

"I know, right?" I said. "It's Bob's new habitat!"

"Great," Fergus mumbled. He gets extra cranky when he's tired. "That's all we need. A cage for a lizard we can't even find."

"Not true," I said. "I found Bob under the house. And also this cool Indiana Jones whip thing!"

I grabbed the rope from the corner of the garage and unwound it, then I whipped it back and forth and it got wrapped around my legs. "Amazing, right?"

"You went under the house?" Mom asked. "All by yourself?"

"I sure did," I said. "Bob was under the house and he needed saving, so I went down there and found him. And this cool rope!"

"Yeah, we get that you found a rope," Amelia said. She took a closer look at the thing we'd built. It was made of long sheets of clear acrylic enclosing the outside and had all kinds of weirdly shaped wooden things inside. The cage wasn't exactly a work of art, but it was definitely interesting. "It's . . . well, it's . . . bigger."

"It sure is," I said. "We could easily fit ten more Bobs in there. He'll never want to leave his cage again. Right, Mr. Gedrick?"

I didn't even wait for Mr. Gedrick to answer. I was so excited I went right into explaining all the power tools we'd used. I explained each one in gory detail—the band saw, the staple gun, the nail gun, and the power drill.

"Stanley used the power tools?" Mom asked. "I'm not sure he's old enough to do that."

"It was all very safe," Mr. Gedrick answered. "We took every precaution."

"And look," I said, holding out my hands. "I still have all my fingers."

"It's a nice habitat, honey," Mom said. "And I'm glad you found Bob. I bet he was lonely down there all by himself."

Fergus was less positive about the whole thing. "Dad wouldn't let me use the power tools until I was twelve. Stanley is like five. It's not fair."

"I'm nine," I said. I looked at Amelia. "Do I look like I'm five?"

"Leave him alone," Amelia said. "You're just mad you didn't find Bob or build him a new place to live. Because you're too busy being a selfish jerk."

"That's enough, Amelia," Mom said. She looked at Mr. Gedrick for some help, but Mr. Gedrick just looked at the whole family with a thoughtful expression. Fergus stormed off, but Amelia patted me on the shoulder. "It's a neat cage. And you look like a nine-year-old to me. How about we do the next project together?"

I felt a warm, fuzzy feeling I hadn't felt in a long time. "Do you think we could get Fergus to help us, too?"

Amelia looked in the direction Fergus had gone, then over at Mr. Gedrick. "Don't get your hopes up, but I'll see what I can do."

"Sweet! Wanna try my new whip?" I asked, holding it out to her.

Amelia put her hands up and shook her head. "No thanks. But I'll tell you this—you guys have given me more inspiration, just the thing I needed."

Mr. Gedrick was noticeably happy about the way Amelia was helping me out. He smiled at her and she nodded as I whirled the whip around my head like a cowboy until it tangled over my shoulders.

Mom went back to her own work and left me, Mr. Gedrick, and Amelia in the garage. Fergus was probably locked away in his room, still wishing for a sandwich, and we all knew better than to go in there.

"Maybe it's time we looked at your plans," Mr. Gedrick said. "The cage was just a warm-up. And it's really quite basic. We need real plans for the big project."

"And we need a real architect," I said. "Like you, Amelia."

Amelia couldn't help but smile. She liked being called an architect.

"Should we have a look?" Mr. Gedrick asked.

Amelia went back to her room and returned with the tube of paper. She looked at Mr. Gedrick like she was afraid she might let him down. "I still need to make some adjustments, but I think it's getting close."

"I'm sure it's amazing," I said. "I wish we could get Fergus in on this. He's really good with the power tools."

"Don't worry about him," Amelia said. "He's such a jerk anyways. We don't need Fergus."

"I'm not so sure about that," Mr. Gedrick said. He put his hands in the pockets of his green felt jacket. "Wouldn't it be better if you all did this together, as a family?"

I could tell Amelia wanted to disagree. Fergus made her crazy. But it obviously meant a lot to Mr. Gedrick.

"We can't make him help us, but it's fine with me if he joins in," Amelia said, and then she turned to the rolled-up tube of paper. "Let's see what you guys think of the plan and we can figure out what to do about Fergus later."

Mr. Gedrick thought about this idea for a second then nodded once.

"I'll need something to hold the corners down," Amelia said as she removed the rubber band from the tube.

"No problem," I said. I left the garage through the side door and went into the backyard. A few seconds later I was back, holding four smooth stones. "Will these work?"

Amelia nodded and went to the workbench, where she unrolled the plans and set one rock on each of the four corners.

"Look at all these lines and all that shading and the measurements!" I said. "This is totally awesome!"

Mr. Gedrick took a long look at the plans. He leaned down close and moved his head from side to side, taking in all the details. When he stood back up straight there was a long pause. Mr. Gedrick took out his field guide and wrote something in there.

"It's ambitious," he said. Another pause and then he looked at Amelia. "But if we can do it, it will be brilliant."

Amelia smiled from ear to ear. She looked like a little light had come on inside her.

"What are we waiting for?" I said. "Let's do this!"

And so we did.

WEEDWACKING AND YARD GNOMES

Fergus had a baseball game the next day and he was looking for a warm-up partner. What I really wanted to do was work on the project in the garage, but Mr. Gedrick said the yard had to be "dealt with" first. Whatever that meant. I could tell my brother was mad because Mr. Gedrick was planning to let me use the power tools, but he ended up letting me play catch with him anyway. I was pretty sure it was because there was no one else to ask, but that was okay. I was kind of surprised he asked me at all, because the truth is I wasn't that great at catching or throwing.

"Fire it in here," I said from one side of the backyard. "I can handle it."

My brother shook his head like he really wished I wasn't his only option. He threw the ball and, man, it was a heater. It nearly took my head off.

"I got a glove on that one!" I yelled as I ran back toward the fence to find the ball. I'd basically jumped out of the way and thrown my glove at Fergus's fastball.

"You can do this, Stanley," Fergus said. "Just toss it right back at me. It's not that hard."

Easy for you to say, I thought. I ran forward two or three steps and launched the ball in Fergus's general direction. The ball sailed up on the roof, rolled to the top of the eave, and disappeared.

"This is hopeless," my brother said.

"Man, did you see how far that went?" I said. "That was awesome."

We walked around to the front of the house and found Mr. Gedrick mowing the lawn.

"Hey, have you ever played catch?" Fergus yelled into the yard. But Mr. Gedrick didn't hear him, so he walked out onto the grass and stood in Mr. Gedrick's way.

"Found it," I yelled over the hum of the mower. The ball had landed in a flowerpot, and I dug it out. I was only a few feet away from Fergus, so I underhanded it to him. It bounced off the lawn mower and landed at his feet.

"Want to play some catch?" Fergus asked, picking

up the ball in case Mr. Gedrick still couldn't hear him. Mr. Gedrick turned off the lawn mower and the two of them stared at each other.

"Hello?" Fergus said, like maybe Mr. Gedrick was in some kind of yard-work trance or something. "Anybody in there?"

Mr. Gedrick walked over to the garage and returned with a Weedwacker. "If you'll help me whip this yard into shape, I'll practice with you. I can catch, you can pitch."

"Hey, I'll run the Weedwacker for free," I said. "Let me at that thing."

I could tell Fergus wanted to say no to Mr. Gedrick's offer. Our yard was in bad shape: dandelions galore, overgrown grass, and flower beds full of weeds. I happened to know for a fact that Fergus hated yard work more than Brussels sprouts, and Brussels sprouts made him want to barf. But showing Mr. Gedrick how fast he could pitch? That would be priceless.

"You got a deal," Fergus said, grabbing the Weedwacker from Mr. Gedrick.

"Foiled again," I said. "What's my job?"

Mr. Gedrick looked around and his eyes landed on the weedy flower beds.

"This is totally lame," I complained, but I went to work anyway.

Unfortunately for us, the yard turned out to be a

much bigger deal than we'd imagined. Right after Mr. Gedrick finished mowing the lawn he went over to Fred and started taking flowers out of the trunk. As Fergus trimmed and I weed pulled, the flowers kept coming. It didn't seem possible that the tiny car could hold so many flowers, but more and more kept showing up.

Fergus finished edging the lawn with the Weed-wacker and the lawn seemed greener than ever. It was like there'd been some yard magic going on here. The whole front of the house looked better than it had in months.

"So, we done here or what?" Fergus asked. He started heading for his glove and ball.

"Not even close," Mr. Gedrick said.

Fergus rolled his eyes. "What kind of deal is this anyway?"

"It's the deal you signed up for," Mr. Gedrick said.

"Come on, Mr. Gedrick. Let's just play some catch already."

But there was no way Mr. Gedrick was catching even a single ball until the yard was finished. He had a little shovel in his hand and started digging a hole in one of the flower beds.

"I'll dig, you two plant," Mr. Gedrick said, and he moved on, digging another hole. "We'll be done in a flick and a sniff, you'll see."

"A flick and a sniff?" Fergus asked.

"Sure," I agreed as I plopped the first yellow flower into my newly weeded area. "A flick and a sniff. Obviously."

Mr. Gedrick was superfast at digging holes and we fell behind. I could feel the sun heating up overhead as I picked a purple flower and stuffed it in one of the holes. No matter how fast we went, there was no keeping up with Mr. Gedrick. It was like he had ten hands, digging holes all around the beds.

We pushed ourselves as fast as we could go. We weren't going to let Mr. Gedrick get too far ahead. Pretty soon we were covered in dirt with sweat pouring from our brows. We were so busy planting we didn't even look up until we heard the sound of water behind us. Mr. Gedrick had dug all the holes and he was following us with a watering can.

"Don't worry," Mr. Gedrick said. "I won't lap you. There wouldn't be anything for me to water if I did."

How was Mr. Gedrick so fast? He put his head down and kept working, and we wound our way around the yard as we felt the pressure of Mr. Gedrick at our heels. Mr. Gedrick swept and tidied and put away all the tools. By the time he returned and finished the watering, we were finally on the last few flowers. When we were done, we stood in the driveway next to him.

I stared into the yard, and Fergus flicked some sweat from his brow. Then he sniffed.

"You see there?" Mr. Gedrick said. "A flick and a sniff and we're all done."

"I knew there would be a flick and a sniff!" I yelled.

"Well now," Mr. Gedrick said, looking at the new yard. "That does look nice."

Fergus and I couldn't believe our eyes. The front yard looked amazing, better than any other yard on the street. Mr. Gedrick had a bag in one hand, and he handed it to Fergus. When Fergus dug inside, he found something that made us laugh out loud.

"Yard gnomes? You gotta be kidding me."

"Sweet," I said. "I love yard gnomes."

Mr. Gedrick set the bag on the sidewalk and took out the two gnomes. One had a yellow hat and a goofy smile on its face. The other one looked a lot like a mini Mr. Gedrick, with a green jacket and a red tie.

"The finishing touch," Mr. Gedrick said. "Like icing on a cake."

Fergus shook his head and went out into the flower beds, where he set them down staring at each other.

"Perfect," Mr. Gedrick said.

One of the neighborhood dads drove by slowly and rolled down his window. "Looking good, guys! Come by my place next!"

I watched as Fergus smiled like he was proud of the work we'd done. I bet he hadn't felt this good since pitching a no-hitter in a playoff game two seasons ago.

"There is one more thing I'd like to add," Mr. Gedrick said. "It would be a little bit of work, but I think it would be worth it."

Fergus grabbed me by the shoulder and we walked off into the middle of the yard together. We bent over with our hands on our knees, like we were a team setting up a play.

"This could go on all day," Fergus whispered. "I think we should bail."

"Yeah, but what about showing Mr. G. how fast you can pitch?" I asked. "I'd love to see his face when one of those burners hits his glove."

Fergus seemed to be daydreaming about one of those pitches, too.

"Don't say I didn't warn you when we end up out here until dark," Fergus said.

"Let's see what he wants to do," I suggested. "If it's a ton of work, we can always huddle up again."

I stood and clapped my hands and said, "Break!" Then we walked back over to where Mr. Gedrick was waiting.

"Okay, we'll bite," Fergus said. "What have you got up that green sleeve of yours?"

Mr. Gedrick walked toward the front door without a word. When he arrived on the porch he turned back. "Are you coming or not?"

Mr. Gedrick didn't wait for an answer as he opened the front door and stepped through.

"This guy is so confusing," Fergus said, but we followed anyway.

When we got into the house, Mr. Gedrick was missing. We checked the kitchen, but we only found Mom hunched over her table. So we went down the hall toward the bedrooms. There we saw something we hadn't seen before: Mr. Gedrick's door was open.

"Whoa," I said.

"Hey, Mr. G., you in there?" Fergus asked. We walked a few more steps down the hallway, and Mr. Gedrick's head popped out.

"That's close enough, I'll bring the parts to you," he said.

"The parts for what?" Fergus asked.

Mr. Gedrick appeared, and he was carrying a big slab of painted plywood with all sorts of shapes cut into it. It was mostly blue and green with a little yellow here and there. He carried it to where we were standing and set it on the shag carpet.

"It's too heavy for one of you," Mr. Gedrick said. "You'll both need to carry it out."

We looked at the piece of wood. It was about four

feet tall and five feet long. Stars and moons and comets had been carefully cut out, so it looked like a bunch of cookie cutters set on a countertop.

"What the heck is this crazy thing?" I asked. "And where did it come from?"

Mr. Gedrick looked like he wanted to go back and get more parts, but he also looked worried his helpers might quit on him, and he couldn't have that.

"Do you remember that night when I made all that noise?" Mr. Gedrick asked. We nodded, so Mr. Gedrick went on. "I built some parts. This is one of them."

"Parts for what?" Fergus asked.

"You'll see," Mr. Gedrick said. "In due time."

Mr. Gedrick went back to his room to get more parts and left us in the hallway holding the piece of wood with all the cutouts.

"Should we huddle up again?" I asked.

"I'm kind of curious where this is going," Fergus said. "Aren't you?"

"You bet I am," I agreed.

It took us seven trips to bring all the parts out into the front yard. We stacked them up against the big tree next to my tire swing. There were a bunch of different shapes and sizes. Lots of cutouts were in the wood.

"Okay, Mr. Gedrick," Fergus said as he caught his breath. "We're not lifting another finger until you tell us what all this crazy stuff is for."

Mr. Gedrick walked over to his tiny red car and opened the trunk again, ignoring Fergus. He pulled out three hammers and a bag of nails. When he came back, he handed each of us a hammer and looked up at the tree. It was a tall tree with a wide base and a top full of green leaves.

"It's for the tree house, of course," Mr. Gedrick said. "First we need to nail in the ladder so we can get up there."

"A tree house!" I yelled. "I love tree houses!"

"That does sound pretty cool," Fergus agreed, but I think he thought it would be great for *me*. My big brother, helping make a tree house for *me*? Had an alien jumped into his body?

Mr. Gedrick picked up one of the ladder rungs and started nailing it to the tree.

"Do you need me to teach you how to use a hammer?" Mr. Gedrick asked.

"Heck no," Fergus and I said at the same time. Then Fergus added: "I've been hammering for years. Stand aside, nanny."

Mr. Gedrick picked through the ladder rungs, rapped one with his knuckles three times, and handed it to Fergus.

"Be my guest," Mr. Gedrick said.

Fergus took a nail and began pounding it into the wood, but it bent sideways about halfway through the rung.

"Dang it," Fergus said, and picked up another nail.

He hammered harder this time, really whaling on it, and the same thing happened.

"You bought crummy nails," Fergus said. "They keep bending over."

"Really now?" Mr. Gedrick said, acting all concerned. He picked up two more nails, tapping them lightly into the rung several times. A second later the rung was secured to the tree.

Fergus grabbed the rung, putting everything he had into yanking it off the tree. But it stayed there, like it had been welded in place with a blowtorch.

"Don't hit it quite so hard," Mr. Gedrick said, handing Fergus another rung. "It's not like hitting a home run. More like a single."

Fergus rolled his eyes, but he took it slower this time and the nails went through the wood much more easily.

"That's the ticket," Mr. Gedrick said.

I got a turn and it took me about ten minutes to nail one rung to the tree. But it was the last one, so that felt like progress.

"Now get up in the tree, I'll hand up the floor."

We got up there and went to work. I imagined how excited Mom and Amelia would be to find this perfect tree house sitting up in the tree, but then Fergus hit his thumb with the hammer and he started grumbling again.

"This better not screw up my catching hand. No tree house is worth that much."

"I've hit my thumb many times building things," Mr. Gedrick said, giving Fergus a thumbs-up sign. "They always bounce back."

Fergus grumbled some more, but he went back to hammering.

"There's another tree in the backyard," Mr. Gedrick said. "But it's not doing too well."

We stopped working and stared down at Mr. Gedrick.

"My dad planted it a long time ago," Fergus said. "But it died. Mom's talked about cutting it down, but I think it's got sentimental value or something."

"Has it been dead for many years?" Mr. Gedrick asked.

"A couple years, at least. Dad was good at a lot of things. Trees wasn't one of them."

"I see," Mr. Gedrick said. He took out his field guide and made a note while we stared down at him.

We kept building and after a while there were walls on two sides. By the time the third wall went up, I was hammering like a champ and so was Fergus.

"You know who's really going to love this thing?" Fergus asked.

"The neighborhood cats?" Mr. Gedrick answered as he hoisted up the last wall.

"Very funny. I would have loved one when I was Stanley's age. You're going to dig this, aren't you, Stanley?"

"It's like a clubhouse," I said, thinking about all the fun stuff I could do up there. "Probably no girls allowed, but us guys can sort baseball cards and spy on the neighbors. And eat candy."

"I was thinking the same thing," Mr. Gedrick said. "How good it is that you're building it together."

When the walls were up, Fergus looked through the open top at the leaves and the sky.

"How are we going to get the ceiling on this masterpiece? Bet you didn't think of that, Mr. Brilliant."

Mr. Gedrick smiled one of his half smiles and put his hand on one of the walls. When he pulled his hand away, we saw that the wall hinged, leaving a giant open window in its place.

"There's one on your side, too," Mr. Gedrick said.

It didn't seem possible, but when Fergus reached over he found he could lift the top half of the wall up toward the sky.

"You really thought of everything," Fergus said. "Impressive, Mr. G."

The two sides met in the middle, and Mr. Gedrick pulled four wooden pins out of his pocket. He placed them in holes on two of the walls, and the pins held up the ceiling.

"This way, if you want a skylight, all you have to do is fold down the walls," Mr. Gedrick said.

We looked out the big window on one side and listened to the birds in the tree. Then Fergus looked at me. "I'm actually happy for you, runt."

"It's the best tree house ever," I said.

"It's a little small for me," Mr. Gedrick said as he sat with his knees in his chest. "But it will be just right for you two. You know, Fergus, it might be useful to try some new nicknames that are not runt or dweeb."

Fergus laughed and shook his head. "I'll see what I can do, Mr. G."

Mr. Gedrick looked at Fergus and offered a half smile. "And now we are finished and I owe you some baseball."

"No way," Fergus said. "Not until we show this to everyone else."

We climbed out of the tree house with big, dumb smiles on our faces. Then we raced each other across the yard and into the house, screaming for

Mom and Amelia. I grabbed Mom by the hand and pulled her out of her chair, and Fergus took off down the hallway to find Amelia.

"Come on, you've got to see this!" I said as I pushed Mom toward the front door onto the porch. Mom tried to ask me where we were going, but I didn't answer. It had to be a surprise.

When Fergus showed up with Amelia, he swept his hand across the front yard and pointed up into the tree house.

"Check it out! I did all this!"

Mr. Gedrick was trimming the hedge with some pruning shears. He looked up and nodded, then returned to his trimming.

"A tree house!" I shouted. "Amazing, right?"

I was gone in a flash, running across the yard and climbing the ladder. When I reached the top, I looked out one of the big windows and waved down at everyone.

"Fergus," Mom said, completely surprised by the new yard and the tree house. "You did all this?"

"Yeah, most of it. Mr. Gedrick helped me some. And Stanley."

Fergus looked at Mr. Gedrick and seemed to remember the lesson about not exaggerating. "Actually, this is one nanny who's really good with yard tools and hammers. It was a total team effort. And Stanley helped a ton. We all did it together."

Looking up from the hedge, Mr. Gedrick seemed truly pleased.

"Are those yard gnomes?" Amelia asked. "That one looks just like Mr. Gedrick. That's funny."

"Everything is wonderful," Mom said. "Thank you, Fergus and Stanley. And thank you, Mr. Gedrick."

Mr. Gedrick nodded and smiled. "All in a day's work, Ms. Darrow. The boys were a big help."

"Hey, Fergus, you should help us with our project in the garage," I yelled from high up in the tree. "We could really use a speed demon like you with the power tools."

Fergus looked around the yard and over at Mr. Gedrick. "I'll think about it. But first, Mr. G. promised me some baseball."

Mr. Gedrick stopped snipping and clipping and looked up at all of us. Nothing seemed to make him happier than when we were willing to work together and help each other out.

"You've got that game tomorrow," Mr. Gedrick said. "Let's practice your pitching first. I'd like to see that fastball for myself."

"Be careful what you wish for," Fergus said. "I'm going to bring the heat."

"I expect nothing less."

Amelia glanced up at me, looking a little hurt for some reason. "Come on, Stanley. We've got our own work to do."

"You go ahead," I said. "I want to see Fergus throw some heat."

Amelia shoved her hands in her pockets. "Fine, do whatever you want."

"I can't believe I have a tree house!" I said.

Mom threw an arm around Amelia and pulled her in close. I could hear them from my spot up above and I thought again about what a great spy shack the tree house was going to be.

"How about you and me grab a snack and take a break?" Mom asked.

"Really?" Amelia said. "Are you sure you can spare the time?"

"I'm totally lost in the weeds, just like I was in our old yard," Mom joked. "I could use a break."

"Hang on, guys," I said as I climbed down the ladder. "I'll get my glove!"

I ran off to get my glove, Mom and Amelia left for the kitchen, and Mr. Gedrick went back to his clipping and snipping at the hedge.

Mr. Baseball

Mr. Gedrick stepped over to Fred and opened the trunk again. He took out several things as Fergus and I watched: an old baseball glove, a baseball bat, and a baseball cap.

"How does he fit so much stuff in there?" I asked.

"It's a mystery, like Bigfoot," Fergus said. "Completely nuts."

Mr. Gedrick put his baseball cap on and took off his green felt jacket. "The yard is in such good shape. Shall we walk to the park? I'd hate to trample the flowers."

The neighborhood park was just around the block, so Fergus and I agreed. While we walked, Mr. Gedrick rolled up the sleeves on his white shirt. Fergus had never seen him do this before, and it seemed to get him even more excited. Mr. Gedrick might be good at digging holes, but he had no idea what he was in for. Fergus had a fastball that made his catchers shake their hands from the sting.

We arrived at the park and Mr. Gedrick suggested we play a game. We would take turns pitching and hitting and catching.

"I might kill Stanley with my fastball," Fergus said. "But I've got to throw my heat if you're batting. Otherwise it won't be fair."

"Oh, I won't be batting," Mr. Gedrick said. "It will be just you and Stanley."

"Don't worry about me," I said. "I've been lifting weights. Check this out."

I flexed my muscles and nothing happened.

"Your funeral," Fergus said with a shrug.

The game was set up and Fergus pitched first. Mr. Gedrick played catcher, but he didn't let me into the batter's box at first. I think he wanted to see what kind of pitcher Fergus was.

"You sure you're ready for this, old man?" Fergus asked.

"Fire away," Mr. Gedrick said. He got down in the catcher's position and held his glove out.

Fergus sniffed the air and straightened his cap. He

lifted his left leg and turned his body right, coiling up all his power, and shifted forward. The ball left his hand with a snap of his wrist.

It popped like the sound of a gunshot in Mr. Gedrick's glove.

"Let's see if you can put a little more mustard on it," Mr. Gedrick said as he tossed the ball back to Fergus, but I could tell he felt the sting in his palm.

"Come on, Fergus, hit him with the real stuff!" I shouted. I swung the bat as hard as I could through the air and it nearly knocked me off my feet.

Fergus fired again, even faster, and this time it sounded like a firecracker hitting Mr. Gedrick's glove.

"I really thought you'd have more zip," Mr. Gedrick said. "But you're just getting warmed up. Give it a few more tries."

Mr. Gedrick's hand had to be killing him, but he wasn't going to let Fergus know that.

"I'm warmed up," Fergus said. Fergus was throwing fire and he knew it. He understood the game Mr. Gedrick was playing. "Get in there, Stanley. Time to meet your maker."

I wasn't nervous about getting hit. If there's one thing I know about my big brother, it's that he has uncanny accuracy. I was 100 percent sure I was going to strike out in three, but at least I would live to tell about it.

"Ready, grandpa?" Fergus taunted Mr. Gedrick.

Mr. Gedrick nodded. "I wonder, should we place a wager?"

"You mean like a bet?" I asked as I turned to Mr. Gedrick.

"I do," Mr. Gedrick replied. "How about three pitches for each of you. If Stanley hits one the farthest, he wins. And if Fergus hits the farthest, he wins. I'll abstain."

Fergus laughed and nodded—he's all for a bet he knows he can't lose.

"Mr. Gedrick," I said. "Could I talk to you for a second? Privately?"

I leaned down and whispered, close to Mr. Gedrick's ear. "That's a terrible bet. I can't hit Fergus, it's impossible. I can barely hit it off a tee."

"Nothing is impossible, Stanley. Remember what we agreed on? Just because you're small doesn't mean you can't do big things."

"Yeah, but it's *Fergus*. I've never hit one of his fastballs."

"Never say never," Mr. Gedrick said. "And listen, take your time. Wait for your pitch. Don't rush. Can you remember those things?"

I nodded, but I was sure it would never work. "You got it, Mr. Gedrick. Just don't get mad when I strike out."

"I won't. Because you're not going to strike out."

I felt a surge of confidence. I had lifted the bar off my chest. I had crawled under the house all by myself. Maybe I really could hit a Fergus fastball.

"If I win, you help me and Amelia with the project in the garage," I yelled at Fergus.

"And *when* I win, you do *all* my chores for a month," Fergus yelled back.

I put my hand on my heart like I'd been struck by a Fergus fastball. "Ouch. That one hurt."

I took one more look at Mr. Gedrick, who nodded at me, and then I moved tentatively into the batter's box. "You got a deal."

Fergus laughed again. "Oh man, this is going to be the easiest win ever. Sorry, little bro, but you asked for it."

Fergus took a long look at the plate and started his windup. I looked down and saw Mr. Gedrick flick his glove up toward the sky, then back into position. Fergus let the ball fly. It sailed up over Mr. Gedrick's head, hit the side of a tree, ricocheted sideways, and landed next to a swing set on the playground.

I swung anyway.

"Ah man, I had that one," I said.

Fergus was rattled. He never threw wild pitches, and that one had been completely crazy.

"Wait for your pitch," Mr. Gedrick told again, and then he pulled another baseball out of somewhere—his pocket?—it's hard to say. But he had another one and threw it to Fergus.

Fergus took a deep breath. "One strike. Two more and it's chore city, kiddo."

Fergus skipped his usual start-up routine—sniffing the air and straightening his cap. He went straight into his windup, and this time Mr. Gedrick flicked his glove toward the ground, then back up again. The pitch hit the grass about two feet in front of Fergus, bounced several times, and stopped about halfway to the plate.

I swung so hard I spun around in a circle and fell on my butt. "Did I hit it?"

"What the . . ." Fergus shouted. "No way!"

"Time-out," Mr. Gedrick said.

He pulled me aside and got down on one knee while Fergus picked up the ball and grumbled to himself.

"Okay, you're in his head now," Mr. Gedrick said.

"I am?" I asked.

"Well, sure you are. He's afraid you're going to crank one over the left field fence. Just look at the way he's pitching. Now listen to me carefully, Stanley. He's nervous. This next one is going to come in real slow. He just wants to get one over the plate. It's going to be a fat pitch. You just have to wait for it. Can you do that?"

"You got it, Mr. Gedrick. Wait for the pitch to come to me. No problem."

Mr. Gedrick returned to his position. "Time-in."

Fergus concentrated harder than usual. Maybe I *was* in his head and he'd throw a little less heat, just to make sure it went over the plate. As Fergus wound up, Mr. Gedrick pushed his glove slowly toward Fergus, then back again. This time, the pitch seemed to start out at normal speed, but then, as it came closer to the plate, it slowed way down.

"Wait for it," Mr. Gedrick said as he watched me start to swing too early. "Let it come to you."

Every ounce of my body said swing, but I waited and waited as the ball went slower and slower. By the time it finally reached the plate, it was like the ball wasn't even moving. I saw it hovering in front of the plate, dying to be plastered into the outfield. I finally swung. All my energy went through the bat and connected square on the seam of the baseball with a loud crack that echoed through the park. The ball sailed over Fergus's head and landed somewhere out in the grass.

"I hit it! I hit it!" I shouted. "I hit a Fergus fastball!"

"This is insane," Fergus said, kicking the grass. He threw his glove on the ground.

"He's rounding the bases, folks!" I said as I ran a baseball diamond pattern around Fergus and returned to home.

Fergus started to walk out into the field to get the

ball, but Mr. Gedrick called him back.

"I have another one," Mr. Gedrick said, pulling out a third ball.

"Where do you keep those things?" I asked.

Mr. Gedrick ignored my question. "Nice hit, Stanley. You really clobbered that thing."

I put on my glove and slapped my fist into it a couple of times. "Let's see what kind of stuff you've got."

Fergus passed Mr. Gedrick on his way to home plate and wouldn't look at him. "I hope you can really throw, 'cause I can hit a lot farther than that."

"Send one in here, Mr. G.," I said. "I can handle it."

"I'd prefer not to warm up," Mr. Gedrick said.

Fergus stepped into position and waited for the first pitch. I was sure Mr. Gedrick wouldn't have any speed so I wasn't worried about having my hand blown off.

Mr. Gedrick stared at my glove, then he looked up and saw a bird swooping this way and that, then he wound up and let fly his first pitch. It wasn't exactly a flamethrower. But it did have quite a lot of English on it. The ball weaved wide to one side, then cut sharply away from Fergus. It missed my glove by a good three feet, and Fergus swung with everything he had.

"Strike one," Mr. Gedrick said.

"Whoa! That thing was sliding all over the place," I said. I ran back and got the ball.

Fergus was seriously nervous now. He'd never seen a pitch like that—neither of us had. It had incredible movement on it, and I wondered if Mr. Gedrick was using a trick ball. But when I came back with it, Fergus held it in his own hand and threw it to Mr. Gedrick. It acted like a totally normal baseball.

"You learn that trick in Swoghollow?" Fergus asked. "How about you just throw a normal pitch?"

"As you wish," Mr. Gedrick said. He looked directly at me. "Don't move your glove, not even a hair. Do you understand?"

"I got it, don't move my glove," I said.

Mr. Gedrick wound up and threw his second pitch. It went right down the middle, no movement whatsoever, and it was going about a hundred miles per hour. Fergus swung way late. The ball went by so fast it shocked him into stillness.

When the ball hit my glove, it knocked me onto my back, but I sat up and it was in my glove.

"I got it!" I yelled. "Also my hand feels like it was just run over by a monster truck. Ouch."

"Sorry, Stanley," Mr. Gedrick said.

"This isn't fair!" Fergus said. "You didn't tell me you could pitch like that."

"You didn't ask," Mr. Gedrick said.

Fergus was so mad he looked like he wanted to punch a tree. How was this happening? Baseball is the one thing he's really good at, and Mr. Gedrick was making him look like a fool. He probably wanted to go back to the yard and stomp on all the stupid flowers we had just planted. I bet he wanted to take the baseball bat to those dumb yard gnomes.

"You still have one more try," Mr. Gedrick said. "Stay relaxed. I'll throw the same fastball as last time."

Part of Fergus was definitely happy to hear this—at least he knew what was coming across the plate. But he'd never hit a ball going that fast in his life.

"Concentrate," Mr. Gedrick said. "You can hit this pitch."

"Yeah, Fergus," I said. "You can totally hit it."

Fergus looked down at me. "Thanks, little bro."

"Here it comes," Mr. Gedrick said. He didn't warn me this time. He didn't tell me to keep my glove perfectly still. It's like he knew the ball would never make it to my glove.

Fergus timed it perfectly, slamming the ball so hard it left the park entirely. It sailed over the park fence and into someone's backyard, never to be seen again.

"Wow wow wow!" I shouted. "That would have

been a homer at Wrigley Field! You destroyed it!"

"I guess I did, didn't I?" Fergus said.

Mr. Gedrick walked up and the three of us stood together. He looked up again at the birds flying around over the trees.

"Well, Stanley," Mr. Gedrick said. "I guess you'll be doing some extra chores for a while."

"It's okay. I'd do extra chores for a year to see another hit like that. It's blowing my mind!"

Fergus threw his head back and laughed. "Your hit was really good, too. You timed that one perfectly."

"Thanks, Fergus," I said. My big brother was paying attention to me, even complimenting me. It was the best feeling in the world.

"I tell you what," Fergus said. "I'll do my own work around the house. And I'll help you and Amelia with your project. But you gotta do something for me."

"Anything!" I said.

"Keep coming out here and practicing with me. I could really use a warm-up partner."

I could hardly believe my ears. "You *so* have a deal."

"Stanley, would you do me a favor and go find that ball over by the swings?" Mr. Gedrick asked.

I didn't even answer. I just ran off smiling and laughing and jumping around like a monkey.

When I got back, Mr. Gedrick was staring at Fergus,

his head tilted slightly to one side. "That was a good thing you did there."

Fergus shrugged. "It's not fair for Stanley. I'm bigger and faster and all that. I ought to be able to help my own brother out a little bit."

"He looks up to you, don't you, Stanley?" Mr. Gedrick asked.

"I sure do."

"And Stanley misses your dad the same as you do. I hope you'll remember that."

Fergus didn't seem to know what to say, so he nodded and offered a half smile.

We all walked back to the house together, under the dome of leafy trees and the sun shining through.

Mr. Gedrick didn't talk too much, because I was talking and replaying everything over and over as we went. I played it all again like a famous sportscaster.

Looking at Mr. Gedrick and Fergus laugh at my commentary and thinking about the new tree house, I couldn't remember the last time I'd been that happy.

The next few weeks raced by and before I knew it, we were in mid-July. The yard looked great, we were all arguing less, and us kids were working together on the big project. Even Mom seemed to feel better about her work, although she still didn't think she'd found her inspiration.

The longer Mr. Gedrick stayed, the more he seemed like he was part of our family. I started to worry what it would be like if he ever left.

How would we survive without him?

THE CHICAGO CHAIN SAW DISASTER

Things were going gangbusters in the garage and we were making some serious progress on the big project. I didn't get to use the power tools as much as I wanted to, but I got to use them some. Fergus was cool about helping me out, and he was even getting along with Amelia. They hadn't thrown insults at each other for the whole day, a small miracle. I went out to the backyard to take a break and drink out of the hose, and when I got there, Mom was coming out of the house looking for Mr. Gedrick. He was sitting on a bench, staring at the dead tree.

"Hey, Mr. Gedrick," I said. "Why are you hanging around in our boring backyard?"

"Waiting for someone to arrive."

This sounded mysterious and I asked him who he was waiting for, but before he could answer, Mom showed up.

"Oh, there you are," Mom said. "I've been trying to find you."

"My apologies," Mr. Gedrick said. He winked at me, like the waiting part was over. "I was just looking at this tree, wondering why it's here."

Mom stepped out onto the patio and folded her arms across her chest. "We probably should have cut it down years ago, but Jonathan planted it."

The tree only had one dried-up leaf on it, way up in the empty branches. It seemed to be holding on to the dead tree for dear life.

"It might be time to let it go," Mr. Gedrick said.

The tree had been this way for two years now. My dad didn't have it removed because he always hated to let things go that might someday have a purpose or come back to life. It always bothered Mom to see the tree, like it was something Dad had left behind that he should have taken with him. Instead he'd left it there for her to deal with, like a lot of other things.

"Maybe you're right," Mom said. "We should cut it down."

Mr. Gedrick's left eyebrow went up a little.

"Could you make sure the kids are occupied this morning?" Mom asked. "Huxley is coming by soon and I really need to stay focused."

"Consider it done," Mr. Gedrick said.

Mom went back to work and Mr. Gedrick stood up. He took out his pointer and extended it, staring up into the blue sky at the lone leaf hanging from the dead tree. He whipped the pointer to one side and a burst of wind flew through the empty branches.

"Whoa," I whispered.

The dead leaf flapped and flopped in the breeze and came loose, falling toward the yard. Mr. Gedrick caught it on the end of his pointer and it stayed balanced there. Then he tossed the leaf in the air with the pointer, caught it in his free hand, and closed his fist around it. When he opened his hand, the leaf had been pulverized into a thousand dried-out pieces. Another soft breeze blew in and the pieces scattered away on the wind.

"It's time," Mr. Gedrick said. He stared at the dead tree.

"Time for what?" I asked.

"We shall see," Mr. Gedrick said.

His answer made no sense to me, but that was normal, especially when something that seemed like magic was happening. He was most mysterious during times like those.

"Important meeting in the backyard," he said. "Do me a favor and gather the troops?"

"Sure thing," I said.

I ran to Amelia's room, where she was working on more parts of the plan. It had gotten bigger and bigger, so we needed lots of drawings.

"Important meeting in the backyard with Mr. Gedrick, posthaste," I said, trying to sound like Mr. Gedrick.

I didn't wait for an answer, heading for Fergus's door with the same message. He was taking a break from the garage to watch baseball highlights.

"What's this all about?" Fergus asked Amelia when they were both in the hallway.

"There's no telling with Mr. Gedrick," Amelia responded.

"I hope it's not more yard work," Fergus said.

"Maybe we get to play more baseball," I guessed as we started through the house. "Or build a robot."

I rubbed my hands together excitedly. We walked through the kitchen just as the doorbell rang, and Mom hurried us into the backyard and told us to stay outside.

"Why do I suddenly feel like we're a pack of dogs?" Fergus asked.

"Just go," Mom said while she pulled her hair into a ponytail and went to the door.

We all arrived in the backyard, but there was no Mr. Gedrick to greet us.

"Are you sure he wanted to meet us here?" Amelia asked me. "I'm not in the mood for playing catch, plus I have a lot of work to do. We're in the details now with the project. It takes planning."

"That's weird. He told me to meet him out here just a second ago," I said. "You guys stay here, I'll go find him."

I went back into the kitchen just as Huxley and Mom were coming in the front door.

"The property is looking very nice," I heard him say as they walked through the living room, looking all around. "And this place—wow, Elsa. You're really getting the hang of this domestic-duty thing. I hope your work on our little project is half as good."

"I'm learning to juggle," Mom said as she guided Huxley into the kitchen. "And Mr. Gedrick is very helpful. He's our nanny."

"I'd call him a miracle worker," Huxley said as he entered the gleaming kitchen.

"Have you guys seen Mr. Gedrick?" I asked when they came in. Mom seemed surprised to find me standing in the kitchen.

"The last time I saw him he was outside," Mom said. "How about you go out there and look for him?"

"Sure thing, just as soon as I get a snack."

Mom didn't seem to know what to say, but it didn't matter. Huxley jumped right in.

"So, what have you got to show me?" he asked as he hovered over the worktable.

"Well, uh, let's see," Mom stammered. "I've got two exteriors and a few matching interiors I like. How about this to start."

This was getting interesting, so I drifted over by the table to get a look at the designs for the Chicago Community Arts Center. They were all done in colored pencils with lots of drawings and numbers. I munched on some potato chips with a loud crunching sound.

"Hmmmmm," Huxley said.

Mom gulped. It didn't sound good. Huxley looked long and hard at the plans, moving back and forth to get a good view of everything. Finally, after a long time, he smiled.

"I love it," Huxley said with enthusiasm. "It's forward thinking. It's brave. It's exciting. And it's nearly finished."

"Really? If I could just get more time, I'm sure I can do something more inspiring. I've seen buildings like this one all over the country. Are there some changes you'd like to discuss?"

I could tell Mom knew she could do better work. She wasn't very proud of what she'd done so far.

"Could I get a glass of water maybe?" Huxley asked. "It will help me think."

I thought this was a weird thing to say, but Mom went to the cupboard anyway. While her back was turned, Huxley took out his phone and snapped a picture of the plans. Then he flipped to the interiors and snapped those, too. I took this as a good sign—he must have really liked those plans. *Good for you, Mom!* By the time Mom got back with the water, Huxley had picked up the plans and carried them over to the island in the middle of the kitchen.

"The light is better here, and I can lay them all out," Huxley said.

Mom handed him the water.

"Oh no, thank you," Huxley said. "I'm fine."

This was doubly strange, I thought, but Mom didn't say anything as she put the glass down on the counter.

"I'm heading out to the backyard," I said. "Looks like you two have this covered."

Mom smiled nervously and Huxley ignored me. They started reviewing the plans more carefully, and I went back out in the yard and closed the kitchen door behind me.

"There you are," I said as Mr. Gedrick was coming around the side of the house. "I was searching for you in the kitchen. And I got a snack."

Mr. Gedrick was carrying a big box. He set it down in the yard and pulled something out that made my eyes go wide.

"Whoa! What are you going to do with that thing?" I asked.

Mr. Gedrick had a shiny new chain saw in his hands.

"I'm not going to do anything with it," Mr. Gedrick said. "Amelia is."

Fergus started laughing. "She can barely handle a hair dryer. I'll cut down whatever you want. Point the way."

Amelia couldn't stand it when Fergus belittled her, but at the same time, I could tell she definitely didn't want to work the chain saw. "Let Fergus do it. I don't want to."

"What are we cutting down?" I asked. I was more concerned than my brother or sister, because there was really only one thing that needed cutting down in the backyard.

"This tree has been dead a long time," Mr. Gedrick said. "It's time for it to go."

"But my dad planted that tree," I said.

"Your dad created a lot of great things around here, including you," Mr. Gedrick said. "But this tree, it's not something he would have wanted to keep. He would have wanted you to remove it and plant a new one."

"How do you know?" I asked.

Mr. Gedrick took a long, hard look at the tree. "This tree needs to be cut down so we can plant a new life here."

I stared at the tree along with everyone else. "I guess it would be kind of cool to see it fall over."

"Wait until I get my hands on that saw," Fergus said. "This is going to be awesome."

"But Dad planted it," Amelia said as she looked up into the leafless limbs. It was a big tree, at least twenty feet tall. "Shouldn't we keep it?"

"I think Dad would be happy we finally chopped it down," Fergus protested. He was itching to get that chain saw in his hands. "We can plant a new one in the same spot, and dedicate it to Dad."

Amelia nodded timidly. "I guess that could be cool."

Mr. Gedrick knelt down next to Amelia and held out the chain saw. "Being a family is more than making plans. We need you to go on the journey with us."

Amelia stepped back and looked at Mr. Gedrick with her mouth half-open. If there was one thing I knew about my sister, I knew she liked to go it alone. She'd never been much for doing things together, and Dad had always said the same kind of thing: *we need you to come along with us.* Good old Mr. Gedrick, whipping out the magic words right when we needed them.

"I don't want to do it," Amelia said.

"How about if we do it together?" Mr. Gedrick said. "I'll help you."

"Did I mention she can barely handle a hair dryer?" Fergus repeated.

That sealed the deal for Amelia. She looked just mad enough to cut down a tree with a chain saw.

"Fine," she said to Mr. Gedrick. "I'll do it."

Fergus shook his head and grumbled. "This ought to be real interesting."

Mr. Gedrick took Amelia to the base of the tree and explained how the chain saw worked. He gave her a pair of clear glasses to wear, so none of the wood chips would land in her eyes. And then he pointed out exactly where to put the blade and told her it had to be right there or the tree might fall in the wrong direction.

Amelia fired up the chain saw.

"What in the world is that?" Mom shouted from the kitchen window.

Huxley was a curious person, and he ran to the window to see what was going on.

"Hey, Mom!" I shouted as she pulled the window all the way up.

"Your kid's got a chain saw!" Huxley yelled out the window. "She's cutting down a tree in your backyard. Wow, this is crazy."

Amelia was halfway through the trunk in nothing flat and the tree started to sway.

"Hey," Huxley said, backing up a few steps. "That thing is headed right for us. Your kid is trying to kill me!"

Huxley dove out of sight and Mom jumped to one side. As the tree came down, it broke through the roof and landed somewhere between the island and the stove. I looked at Mr. Gedrick and he flicked his index finger to one side, then the other. Then I looked back through the kitchen window and saw Mom's computer crushed under a branch. The arts center plans were flying up in the air, struck by a branch. They danced down onto the stove. Then the stove turned on, because it had been struck by another branch, and the plans started burning up.

"Fire!" Mom yelled. She was trapped between the wall and the tree trunk, but Mr. Gedrick walked right up the flattened tree, avoiding limbs as he went, and placed his green felt jacket over the small fire. Then he turned the stove off.

There wasn't much smoke, not enough to cause any damage, but Mom's computer and the plans were destroyed. Fergus and I climbed along the tree and jumped down into the kitchen.

"This is bananas," I said.

Huxley stumbled out from under the table, brushing himself off. "That was some very exciting stuff. Really woke me up!"

He saw that the plans had burned up and shrugged his shoulders. "You'll have to start over, I guess. But I'm certain you can do it."

Mom couldn't even speak.

"I'll be back in a week with the big boss," Huxley said, stepping over part of the tree on his way toward the front door. "I'm sure you'll do fine. Let me know if you want to finish up at headquarters. This might not be the best place to work for a while."

Huxley took one more long look around and shook his head. "The only way of finding the limits of what's possible is by going beyond them, into the *im*possible!" Huxley said.

He always said the weirdest things.

"Thank you for those inspiring words," Mr. Gedrick said. He was brushing the ashes off his green felt jacket. Huxley waved off Mr. Gedrick and wandered out toward the living room.

"Boy, that was something else," Huxley said with a laugh. "Wait till they hear about this at the office. Classic."

Fergus and I went to the backyard to find Amelia. She'd been holding the chain saw the whole time, frozen from shock. She set the chain saw down on the grass and looked at the disaster she had caused.

Fergus walked up to her, shaking his head, and I followed close behind. I expected Fergus to yell something mean and lose his marbles, but he surprised me.

"When Mom comes out here, say I cut it down," Fergus said. "I'll take the blame for it."

"No, let me do it," I said. "She won't get as mad if it's the youngest. Right?"

But inside I wasn't so sure. I imagined the rest of the summer spent grounded with no TV, no movies, and no video games.

"Thanks, you guys," Amelia said. "But I can't let you take credit for my catastrophe."

We all looked at the house and shook our heads.

"Wow," I said. "This is bonkers."

"You said it, brother," Fergus agreed.

Mr. Gedrick and Mom came out of the kitchen. The moment I saw Mom I knew it was even worse than I had imagined. She was crying.

"Everything is ruined," she said. "My whole life. It's all ruined."

She continued to cry, and something about the words she said really bummed me out. I knew what she meant. Dad was gone and he wasn't coming back. That was the real problem. It felt like an all-time low. All the progress we'd made had crashed to the ground, just like the tree.

"I'm sorry, Mom," Amelia said. "I cut the tree down. It was my mistake."

"But we helped," I said. "Right, Fergus?"

"We totally helped," Fergus agreed.

Mom sat down on the bench next to the dead tree and shook her head. "I'm glad you're all safe, but what a mess. My plans burned up. And the kitchen . . ." She couldn't come up with anything else to say.

We looked at Mr. Gedrick. We didn't speak. We didn't have to because our expressions said everything we needed to say.

Why did you make us cut down this tree? This is all your fault. You've ruined everything.

A Dream of Days Past

Fergus and Amelia scattered to their rooms, but Mom kept sulking on the bench. Mr. Gedrick took a fine linen cloth from his pocket and began wiping down the felt fabric on his jacket. It cleaned up miraculously well, and he put it back on. Then he sat next to Mom on the bench and stared into the yard. I stayed over by the fallen tree trunk, picking at the bark, and the two of them started talking.

"I sat on this very bench with my husband many months ago," Mom said. "Do you know what he said to me?"

"I do not," Mr. Gedrick answered quietly.

"He told me he didn't think he had a green

thumb, and I agreed with him. The dead tree was strong evidence."

"He was self-aware, it sounds like," Mr. Gedrick said.

"He told me the tree would have to come down some day, but not on that day. Then he said something strange. He said maybe the tree would fall when I least expected it, when I needed it most."

Mr. Gedrick didn't say anything, and after a long pause, Mom kept talking. "I told him I couldn't imagine a time when I would need a tree to fall in my backyard, and yet here we are, these many months later, and the tree has fallen very unexpectedly. I wonder what it could mean. Maybe he's speaking to me from somewhere far away."

Mr. Gedrick put his hand on Mom's, just for a moment. It seemed like he was trying to say something to make her feel better, though he didn't talk. And then he left for the kitchen, leaving Mom and me out in the backyard.

I got up off the stump and sat next to Mom. We looked at the remains of the dead tree. Mom sniffed away a few more tears, and I let one fall down my cheek. She put her arm around me, squeezing me close to her.

"Let's go talk to your sister," she said as she got up and breathed a heavy sigh.

"Seems like a good idea," I said.

We walked through the house and stood in front of Amelia's door. Mom knocked quietly but didn't enter. "Can I come in?"

"Sure, I'm just sitting here being miserable," Amelia answered. "And you know what they say about misery."

Mom opened the door and peeked inside. "It likes company?"

I slipped into the room and leaned against the wall by the door. Amelia was sitting on her bed, looking like she was worried about how much trouble she was in.

"Mind if I sit?" Mom asked.

"Misery likes to sit," Amelia said. "I should know."

Mom flopped down on the bed and let her shoulder fall against Amelia's. "Your dad could never get anything to grow in the yard."

"Remember the gardens he tried to plant?" Amelia asked. "How can anyone fail at tomatoes? I thought that was impossible."

They both laughed, and Amelia let her head rest on Mom's shoulder.

"I'm sorry I cut a tree down and it fell on the kitchen," Amelia said.

"I wanted to thank you," Mom said, and boy did that surprise me.

"For what?" Amelia asked.

"Those plans I had weren't what I really wanted to do," Mom said. "But I would have turned them in anyway. That would have been settling for something lousy when I know I can do better. Now they're gone and I can't get them back, and that's very good news."

"But you'll have to start all over," Amelia said. "Don't you hate when that happens? I hate when that happens."

Mom shook her head. "Sometimes it's hard to let go of things, even if you know you have to."

Amelia hugged Mom, and seeing them there I realized they hadn't hugged in a very long time. Amelia started crying. "I miss Dad," she said. "I miss him a lot."

"I know you do," Mom said. "I miss him, too."

I started feeling crummy and wished I could get in on the hug, but I stayed where I was.

Mom held Amelia by the shoulders and looked at her. "It's okay to go forward, but I know it's hard. It doesn't mean we don't love him or that we will forget him. It just means we want to keep on living. You're like me. You like to be alone sometimes. You like to work on your own things. You like to draw and plan. I like those things about you."

"I like those things about you, too," Amelia said.

"Me, too!" I said. I could only keep my mouth shut for so long.

They both looked up and smiled at me.

"Let's make sure we take time to talk like this more often, okay?" Mom said to Amelia.

Amelia nodded and wiped away a tear. "I think that would be super."

They sniffled and smiled even bigger at each other, and Amelia got a thoughtful look on her face. "Why do you think Mr. Gedrick is so sad?"

I knew what Amelia was talking about; we all did.

"I don't know," Mom answered. "But I have a feeling we're going to find out someday. He's got secrets, but they want to get out. I can tell."

"Sometimes, when we all get along better, he seems less sad," Amelia said. "Do you think that's true?"

"I do. I think it's very true indeed."

I heard a commotion in the kitchen. "What's that?" I asked. "Let's go check it out!"

We all decided we'd better see what was happening. When we got in the hallway, Fergus was just coming out of our room.

"How much trouble did you get into?" Fergus asked Amelia.

"Tons," Amelia said, winking at me. "I don't recommend felling a tree into the house."

"Harsh," I said. "But hey, if you do end up getting grounded, I'll play board games with you all day. No problem."

"And I'll play catch with you in the backyard," Fergus said.

"Actually, she went easy on me." Amelia smiled. "But I'm still going to hold you guys to catch and board games."

Darrow Family Magic

When we arrived in the kitchen, we found Mr. Gedrick putting away his pointer in the inside pocket of his green jacket. The tree was gone, the ceiling was fixed, everything was back to the way it was.

"But this is impossible," Mom said.

"Mr. Gedrick is magic," I whispered to Fergus. "I think he's a warlock."

"I know," Fergus whispered back. "Pretty cool, right?"

"You know it, bro."

"How did you do all this?" Mom asked as she tapped on the countertop to make sure it was real.

"It's a matter of physics," Mr. Gedrick said. "Really

quite simple. Although we do still need to cut that tree into firewood."

He gestured toward the backyard, where the tree lay on its side.

"I'll do it!" I yelled.

Fergus stepped forward and put a hand on my shoulder. "How about we both do it. I don't think Mom would ever forgive us if you lost a finger out there."

"Deal, roomie," I said.

We were about to race each other to the chain saw, but Amelia stopped us. "Maybe Mom could help us finish the plan," she said. "We could all finish it together."

The room went silent as we looked on, waiting and wondering what our mom would say. Amelia took Mom by the hand.

"Will you help us?" Amelia asked.

Mom looked at her table, obviously thinking of the work that needed doing, all that inspiration that wasn't showing up as she tried and tried again.

So she said the only thing that made any sense.

"I'd love nothing more."

Mr. Gedrick said he had stuff to do in his room, and everyone wished he could come help us. But he insisted, so I went into superspy mode and followed after him. It was time I got a look inside my old room, and this seemed like my best shot.

When I got there, it was almost like he wanted me to peek inside. He'd left the door open anyway, so I took it as a sign. I crept closer, and when I got one eye around the doorjamb, I was surprised to find that Mr. Gedrick wasn't in there. I opened the door a little wider and took a step inside, hoping a booby trap wouldn't get me. There was a desk and a blow-up mattress on the floor. The wood on the desk and the chair was polished and there were parts that were brass and copper.

I went to the closet, where six sets of clothing were hung. There were six felt green jackets, six green vests, six red ties, and six crisp white shirts. There were also six pairs of pants, but there were no extra shoes. Apparently Mr. Gedrick only owned one pair of shoes, and he took very good care of them.

"Hello, Stanley," Mr. Gedrick said from behind me. I jumped so high my head nearly hit the ceiling.

"Don't scare me like that!" I yelled, holding my chest.

"I warned you it was dangerous to come in here. At least you didn't fall through the trapdoor on the floor."

"The trapdoor? Oh man."

Mr. Gedrick walked past me and took a small wooden box from the closet. Then he sat down and took his shoes off.

"These are in need of a good cleaning," he said. "No time like the present."

"Is there really a trapdoor?" I asked. I was thinking about the pathway I'd taken into the room and hoping I could follow it back out.

"Maybe there is, maybe there isn't. Who can say?"

Mr. Gedrick opened the small box, took out a brush, and began buffing one of the shoes. The shoe was deep black and shiny, and this seemed to make him happy. He stopped what he was doing and looked at his desk. The field guide was there, full of notes and drawings. I followed his eyes and looked at the desk, too.

"Hey, what's that thing?"

It looked like a small globe sitting on a pedestal, but I was too chicken to walk over and grab it. Mr. Gedrick picked it up and dropped it in his jacket pocket.

"That's for another time, another place," he said.

There was some kind of puzzle to all this, but I couldn't put it together. Mr. Gedrick went back to shining his shoes. I started to feel like maybe he wanted to be alone, so I carefully followed the same way I'd come in until I got to the door. Then I ran for the garage to see what was going on there. I found Mom wandering around in a daze while Amelia and Fergus worked. She looked right at me when I showed up.

"You did all this?" she asked.

"Mr. Gedrick helped," I said. "But he made us do most of the work."

"He's a real taskmaster, that guy," Fergus agreed. "But it was fun. And Amelia's design was kind of amazing, I have to admit."

"Was that a compliment?" Amelia asked.

Fergus shrugged. He looked at Mom. "We still need help to finish it."

"Lead the way," Mom said, and we all crowded around Amelia's plans.

"Oh my," Mom said, surprised at what she saw. "Amelia, this is really good. Wow."

I could tell Amelia was melting from all the praise she was getting, because she couldn't peel the smile off her face.

"Take it easy, Mom," Fergus said. "Any more compliments and her head won't fit through the door."

I laughed and acted like my head was ten times bigger than a normal head. I wobbled around the garage like I could barely hold it up.

"Where do we start?" Mom asked. She was excited to pound nails or cut wood.

The day disappeared in a fog of sawdust and paint fumes. We laughed a bunch as we worked and after a while we all smelled a roast cooking in the kitchen. Tired and covered in grime and paint, we raced into the kitchen and found the table set and a dinner fit for kings and queens.

"I thought you might be hungry," Mr. Gedrick said. He wiped his hands on his apron.

"Let's eat!" I yelled, and we all sat down together.

We talked and joked and laughed and ate until we were so full we couldn't eat another bite.

"Why don't you come out and help us, Mr. Gedrick?" Mom asked. "We're nearly done."

Mr. Gedrick waved her off. "I have many things to do inside the house. I'll come see when it's finished."

I thought this was odd. Mr. Gedrick was like part of the family now. We *wanted* him to help. But he insisted, so we let it go.

When we returned to the garage, I asked everyone to wait before they started working. They all got together and stared at me.

"We have to do something for Mr. Gedrick. He's done so much for us."

"I agree," Amelia said as Fergus nodded. "But what?"

I had my thinking face on, rubbing my chin with one hand. After a second I had an idea.

"We have to work some *Darrow family* magic. I think it's the only kind of magic that will do the trick."

The Plan Revealed

The next morning we did something special for Mr. Gedrick, and then I went down the hallway to find him.

"Hey, Mr. Gedrick!" I yelled from the other side of my old bedroom door. "We have a surprise for you. You'll never guess what it is."

I heard some shuffling around in there, and then the door opened a crack and his green eyeball was staring down at me. "Give me a moment, I'll be right out."

"Don't take too long. Our surprise is getting cold," I said.

Finally, after about two hundred hours, Mr.

Gedrick opened the door and slipped through, clos-ing it behind him.

"Come on, lazybones!" I said, grabbing his hand and pulling him toward the kitchen. "We're going to be late."

"Late for what?" Mr. Gedrick asked.

"Oh no, you don't," I said. "You're not getting me to tell you about the amazing breakfast we made for you."

I stopped in my tracks. "Aw, man. You tricked me!"

"I suppose I did," Mr. Gedrick said. "I'll act sur-prised all the same."

"Thanks!" I said, pulling Mr. Gedrick harder toward the surprise.

When we arrived in the kitchen, everyone was standing around the table beaming and excited.

"Surprise!" they all yelled.

"We made breakfast for *you*," I said as I stood at Mr. Gedrick's side, leaning into him. "What do you think about that?"

Mr. Gedrick sniffed the air and examined the table full of waffles, strawberries, whipped cream, and sausage.

"We shall see," Mr. Gedrick said, but then he laughed. It was the first time I'd ever heard him do that, and we all laughed along with him, because Mr. Gedrick had a laugh that sounded like a duck.

We ate waffles covered in whipped cream and talked about the project in the garage and Mr. Gedrick enjoyed himself very much.

"This is the best breakfast I've had in a long, long time," Mr. Gedrick said. He had whipped cream stuck to the end of his long nose.

"We have an even better surprise," Amelia said. "Unless you want another waffle first."

"No, no," Mr. Gedrick said, patting his stomach like Santa Claus. "Six is my limit."

"I'll clean this up later," Fergus said like it was no big deal.

"*You're* going to clean the kitchen?" Mom asked. "Who are you and where did you hide my son?"

"Har har har," Fergus said.

I jumped out of my seat and pulled on Mr. Gedrick's jacket. "Come on! We finished the project. You have to come see."

Mr. Gedrick wiped the corners of his mouth and the end of his nose. "Lead on, young Darrow—I can hardly wait."

"Close your eyes," I said. "I'll show you the way."

I accidentally pulled Mr. Gedrick into a chair and a table on the way out the door.

"Almost there!" I said.

Mr. Gedrick seemed to know the garage was lower than the kitchen, and when the door opened he stepped down and stood on the concrete.

"Don't open them yet," I said. "Just stay right there for a second."

There was a lot of noise as we moved things around and the lights were turned off and we ran all over the garage doing last-second stuff. I could tell Mr. Gedrick wanted to peek, but he didn't.

"Okay, open your eyes," I said.

The main light for the garage had been turned off. There were white Christmas lights hung in long rows along the ceiling, drooping down like ropes filled with lightning bugs. They all led to the same place—the Airstream trailer—and they came together above the door. The trailer was covered in tiny sparkling lights, too, but they were every color of the rainbow.

Mr. Gedrick's breath caught in his throat, and I wasn't sure why. Was it because of all the amazing work we'd done, or because we were all together, standing in front of him, with big dumb grins on our faces? Even Bob was grinning, resting in my hand.

Behind us, the Airstream had been polished to a shiny silver. It was really old and super new at the same time.

"Welcome to my new office," Mom said. "And thank you for all you did to help make it possible. If it weren't for you, I'd be stuck in the kitchen for the rest of my life."

Mr. Gedrick took two steps forward. He messed up my hair and stared at the amazing new office we'd created.

"It's marvelous," Mr. Gedrick said. "Just marvelous. Can I see inside?"

"You bet!" I shouted. "That's the best part because Mom helped."

Mr. Gedrick walked to the door and opened it.

"I do believe this is the most creative work space I've ever seen," Mr. Gedrick said.

He sat down at the curved desk that was shaped like a big, flat egg. There was a sleek new computer on top of it. We all piled in behind him and were forced to stand close together.

"I'm so glad you like it," Mom said. "I thought you'd be particularly fond of the curtains."

The curtains were made of green felt and they looked warm and soft. The floor was done in red tiles to match Mr. Gedrick's tie, and the surface of the egg-shaped desk was a bright white. On the desk sat a photo of our family, including my dad. Some of Amelia's work was piled up there, too, and the first baseball Fergus had ever hit out of a ballpark.

Mr. Gedrick turned in the swivel chair and looked at all of us. He spoke like he was very happy and very sad at the same time. "The Darrows have found their melody once again."

From somewhere inside his green felt jacket—was it hidden in his sleeve, folded into sections? Who knows? But there it was: the small globe, along with a glass stand for it to sit on.

"May I add something to your desk?" Mr. Gedrick asked.

He set down the glass base, which was thin and clear as water. Then he placed the small globe on the metal pin and gave it a little spin.

SWOGHOLLOW

"Hey," I said, moving in for a closer look. Bob was still in my hand, and the little lizard also stared. "That's just like the big one we have."

"Indeed it is," Mr. Gedrick said. He got up without any warning and walked out of the Airstream. When we all got out into the garage, he was staring at the large globe on the floor.

"What gives, Mr. Gedrick?" Fergus asked. "Why do you have the same globe our dad did, only smaller?"

Mr. Gedrick didn't answer. He went to the large globe and placed his hand on its smooth surface. It was really big, too big for him to get his arms all the way around, and it sat on a pedestal made of wood. The pedestal was like the smaller glass one in the Airstream, with a pin that ran up through the middle and held it in place. Mr. Gedrick spun the globe softly, so it turned one full rotation.

"Stanley," Mr. Gedrick said. "Do you happen to have that rope you found under the house?"

We were all looking at Mr. Gedrick like something big was about to happen.

"Sure I do," I said, turning to Fergus. "Could you hang on to Bob for me?"

Fergus took Bob and I went into the corner of the garage, where I kept the leather rope coiled up on a nail I'd pounded into the wall. I carried it to Mr. Gedrick and held it out.

"Oh, I don't want it," Mr. Gedrick said. "It's yours, and only you can put it to its proper use."

"I don't understand," I said. "You mean like this?"

I looped it back and forth like an Indiana Jones whip. It tangled up in the air and the end landed on Amelia's foot.

"You're really getting good with that thing," Amelia said. "Be careful though. I'd like to keep all my toes."

"What's this all about, Mr. Gedrick?" Mom said.

"Do you see this groove here?" Mr. Gedrick asked, pointing to the middle of the globe. There had always been a deep, empty space that ran around the middle of the globe. It was about an inch wide, cutting the globe into two halves.

"Sure I see it," I said. I had an idea what Mr. Gedrick was thinking, because I had a small collection of yo-yos. I could imagine the rope working on the globe like a yo-yo string.

"I think I know what he's getting at," Fergus said. He took the other end of the rope in his one empty hand. Bob the lizard watched what we were doing like he was actually interested. "Come on, I'll help you."

We all watched as Fergus put the end of the rope into the groove and then started spinning the globe around. The rope got shorter and shorter until the only part left was the little bit in my hand.

"This is so weird," Amelia said, grabbing Mom's hand and leaning into her.

"You'll need to pull as hard as you can," Mr. Gedrick said as he stepped away from the globe. "Give it all you've got."

I thought about how I'd lifted the heavy bar off my chest and how I'd hit a Fergus fastball. I imagined the globe was light as a feather and gripped the end of the rope as hard as I could. I thought Fergus might try to take the rope away from me, but he just nodded and smiled.

"Here goes nothing," I said.

I ran as fast as I could away from the globe, pulling with all my might, and then I flicked the rope at the very end and it released with a snap. I fell on the garage floor and did a barrel roll toward Amelia and Mom. I would have knocked them over like bowling pins, but they jumped out of the way in time.

"Stanley!" Mom yelled.

"It's okay, Mom. I'm fine, see!"

I was back on my feet in a flash. There was no way I was going to miss seeing that globe spin like crazy.

"Whoa," I said. "Check it out."

When Mom and Amelia turned back to the globe, they saw what I saw. Fergus had moved back a few steps and Mr. Gedrick had put his hands in the pockets of his green felt jacket. That was all fairly normal. It was the globe that captured everyone's attention.

The globe didn't slow down like it was supposed to. It sped up, faster and faster, like it might lift right off the ground or explode into a thousand pieces.

"Is this safe, Mr. Gedrick?" Mom asked. She was backing up, holding her arms out like the globe might start rolling all over the garage and squash us.

Mr. Gedrick smiled his half smile. "I'm afraid there's nothing safe about it."

Mom pushed me and Amelia behind her, but we fought to keep watching what was going on.

"Fergus," Mom said. "Get away from that thing!"

Fergus was mesmerized by the spinning globe, staring at it like an alien had landed.

"Something is happening," Fergus said. He acted confused at first, but then he seemed to understand. "It's opening up."

The globe began to slow down, and as it did, it split apart from the top. It broke open slowly, like the slices of an orange, revealing the inside.

Then the globe stopped turning.

"Welcome to Swoghollow," Mr. Gedrick said.

We all stepped in for a closer look and found small roads and houses and buildings. A tiny train rode around the outside, puffing smoke from its engine as it passed a farm full of cows and horses. A tiny world had been hidden inside the globe all this time.

Mom looked at Mr. Gedrick like she knew a secret she hadn't known before. She knew something important.

"What is it, Mom?" I asked.

She looked right at Mr. Gedrick.

"You were Jonathan's nanny, weren't you?"

"Wait just a second here," I said, gaping at Mr. Gedrick. "*You* were my dad's nanny?"

"Taught him everything he knew. We spent a lot of time in Swoghollow. But that was long ago. This is the first time I've seen the place in ages."

Mom laughed like she couldn't believe it. "I thought you were somehow *him*, coming back to tell me something. I thought I was going crazy. But I see it now. He was with you all along. You knew him, just as we did."

We were drawn to Swoghollow like moths to a porch light. I saw Mr. Gedrick's tiny car drive along a tree-lined road as little leaves fell from the trees like snowflakes.

"You knew our dad when he was a kid, like me?" I asked. "He must have loved Swoghollow."

"That he did," Mr. Gedrick said. "Did you know he never had a family of his own? That's a different story, but it's true. I was his caretaker, a stand-in for a real family. But we did have such fun in Swoghollow. As he got older, all he ever talked about was being the best dad in the world. It was all he wanted."

Fergus glanced up at Mr. Gedrick. "He *was* the best dad. You must have done something right."

"I'm surprised he never showed us the inside of this thing before," I said. "It's awesome!"

"I think it was his very special place, just for him," Mr. Gedrick said. "We should all have a place like this in the world, where only we can go to rest and think and remember."

Amelia ran over and wrapped her arms around Mr. Gedrick. She looked up at him. "Did you come with a message from our dad?"

Mr. Gedrick didn't answer right away, but he did hug Amelia back. It kind of seemed like everything Mr. Gedrick had wanted to say had already been said.

"That he loves you," Mr. Gedrick finally sputtered. "And he's very happy you're doing better."

We stood around Swoghollow, laughing and pointing to all the incredible things that could be found there. But Mr. Gedrick was outside the circle, standing by himself. I watched him look at the Airstream and the lights hanging all around and the open globe. He looked back at me and we locked eyes.

"Welcome home," he whispered quietly.

And then the most magical thing happened.

We turned to Mr. Gedrick and attacked him with hugs. He was no longer outside the circle; he was at its center. Maybe he wouldn't be sad about losing the boy who had become my dad anymore. Like all of us, he was finally ready to go forward.

The Return of Huxley Harvold

We talked Mr. Gedrick into staying for a few more days, even though he kept telling us it was time for him to go. He sat on the bench in the backyard a lot, reading a book or watching the sky for signs of rain. We all knew he was going to leave, but no one wanted to talk about it.

On the day Huxley was scheduled to come back to the house, Mom spent the morning in the Airstream. She'd been in there quite a bit during the day, but she'd made us a promise she wouldn't work so much. We'd all gone to some of Fergus's baseball games together and visited the museum where Amelia had shown us all the stuff she was excited about. Mom had helped me lift weights, and spent time with me in Swoghollow. Hours had gone by as we explored all the parts of Swoghollow and made up stories about the things that happened there.

I was in the tree house when Huxley showed up, and he didn't arrive alone. He brought the big boss with him, the founder of the firm. I liked his boss, Mr. Jivins. He used to show me around the place whenever I went to visit Mom at her old office. He even took me on the roof once. It was windy up there.

Under his arm, Huxley carried a rolled-up set of plans. I watched both guys as they stood on the front porch.

"As I said," Huxley told Mr. Jivins. "I gave Ms. Darrow a lot of ideas to work on." Huxley tapped on the plans under his arm and winked like an idiot. I started to think maybe he'd gotten someone else to work on the same project.

Mr. Jivins was a tall guy but no older than Huxley. He wore an all-gray three-piece suit. "I hope we don't have to let her go."

Huxley raised his eyebrows with a look of concern, but I could tell he was faking it. This guy had something up his sleeve and I hoped it wouldn't mean Mom would be jobless by the time they left.

"Don't be alarmed by the kids," Huxley said. "They're a bit unruly. And the house may be in some disorder, especially the kitchen. Her life is . . . complicated."

"But you can execute your ideas with a different team if necessary?" Mr. Jivins asked.

"Oh yes, very much so," Huxley replied. "And don't forget, the plans are really mine. Elsa Darrow is but the hands that do the masters' work. Shall we knock?"

What a crock of cow pies, I thought. *Who does this guy think he is?*

"Howdy, Mr. Jivins," I yelled from the tree house. Then I climbed down to the yard. I was on the porch in like three seconds flat.

"Stanley Darrow," Mr. Jivins said. "It's always a pleasure to see you. Nice tree house."

"I know, right? I keep all my baseball cards up there, in case you want to check them out."

Mr. Jivins looked like he did want to check them out, but Huxley spoiled the fun.

"I think we better go inside and get on with it. Time is money, as you know, Mr. Jivins."

I walked right past them both and opened the front door.

"Mom's all ready for you. Boy, are you guys going to be happy."

"You know, Stanley," Huxley said awkwardly. "Mr. Jivins is the president of the firm."

"Nice to meet you, prez," I said, and held out my hand. It bugged me that Huxley didn't know Mr. Jivins and I already knew each other.

Mr. Jivins leaned down and played along, shaking my outstretched palm. "The pleasure is all mine, Stanley. Could you find your mother for us? We'd be grateful."

"Right this way," I said as I guided them into the house. "She's out in the garage. Thataway."

I pointed toward the kitchen and started walking, glancing back at Huxley. He was obviously surprised by how tidy the house looked, but when we reached the kitchen, he was downright flabbergasted.

"But I was only here a week ago," he said. "How did this get cleaned up so fast?"

I leaned in and whispered like I was going to tell them both a big secret. "I have no idea."

The two of them stared at me, and Huxley laughed nervously.

"Thisaway," I said as I went to the door leading to the garage. The globe was shut so they couldn't see Swoghollow. Mr. Gedrick and Fergus were standing next to each other, at full attention like army recruits.

"Nice to see you, Mr. Harvold," Mr. Gedrick said. "And who might this be?"

Mr. Jivins was introduced, and Mr. Gedrick nodded

at both men and said, "Welcome to the Darrow home. Shall we begin?"

Huxley looked around the garage like he had no idea what was going on. "Uh . . . sure. Let's . . . *begin?*"

"Very well," Mr. Gedrick said. "If you'll follow me over here, the presentation will start momentarily."

"What's going on?" Mr. Jivins asked Huxley in a whisper that everyone heard.

Huxley shrugged. "Uncharted waters."

He was probably hoping the situation wouldn't get so weird that Mr. Jivins would wonder why Huxley had ever hired Mom in the first place.

Fergus, Mr. Gedrick, and I stood in front of the Airstream and Mr. Gedrick took out his pointer. He extended it into a long silver shaft and tapped on a button next to the door that led inside. The entire front of the Airstream slid sideways on rollers, revealing the inside of the camping trailer.

Mom looked up from her desk. "Oh, are we beginning? And is that Mr. Jivins? Thank you so much for coming. Give us one more second. We're almost finished."

Huxley looked at Mr. Jivins sideways, but Mr. Jivins didn't look back. "Always good to see you, Elsa. I'm looking forward to this. Whatever it is."

Mom punched furiously into her computer. Amelia was standing behind her pointing to things on the screen and offering last-second ideas.

Mr. Jivins leaned toward Huxley and whispered again. I don't really know why he whispered all the time. Everyone could hear him anyway. "Who's designing this project, the kid or the adult?"

"It is highly unusual," Huxley said. "Maybe we should leave."

"No, no. I'd like to see where this is going. And I've always liked Elsa Darrow."

Mom tapped a few more keys, and then she stopped. "There. All done."

"Cutting it rather close, ladies," Mr. Gedrick said, and then he swished the pointer across the top of his head and all the lights in the garage went out.

"Oh my," Mr. Jivins said. "This *is* exciting."

A second later a beam of light appeared from inside the Airstream, projecting like a movie onto the far wall.

"Did anyone bring popcorn?" Huxley asked as a joke, but no one laughed. I handed both Huxley and Mr. Jivins bags of popcorn.

"If only I had a chair to sit on, I'd be as happy as a clam," Mr. Jivins said.

Mr. Gedrick had already thought of this, and before Mr. Jivins could make the full request a chair was bumping the back of his knees. Two folding chairs awaited him and Huxley.

Mr. Jivins smiled and laughed at what a great time he was having. He ate some popcorn. "On with the show!" he yelled.

"I think we've already seen the best part," Huxley mumbled.

The design for the Chicago Community Arts Center began to unfold, and it was even better than I thought it would be. And I thought it would be super-amazing-fantastic-and-great. Mom and Amelia took turns explaining as the building appeared: a globe cut open from the top, its six wings slicing out just like Swoghollow. The six sections were connected by bridges, each of them housing a different area of exciting creative opportunity.

"Each wing extends from the center, like slices of an apple or an orange," Mom said. "So each wing is separate, but it's all part of the same whole."

"And Mom—er, Ms. *Darrow*—has figured out all the engineering," Amelia explained proudly. "The bridges that extend across the middle of each wing aren't just exterior walking paths, they're also structural beams that hold everything together."

"The six wings cover everything Chicago kids need to grow creatively," Mom continued. "Arts and crafts, painting, sculpture, modern art, the classics, and multimedia. As you can see, each of these areas has space for hands-on learning, galleries, and classrooms."

Mom and Amelia explained it so well I couldn't wait to go there myself, and I don't even like art. They talked about the restaurants and the bathrooms, calling the whole thing a "singular experience."

When they were done, the lights came up and Mr. Jivins took another handful of popcorn.

"Well, I must say this is all very exciting," Mr. Jivins said, turning to Huxley. "I'm afraid it's a little bit better than your plans, Huxley. You'd have to agree?"

Huxley had no idea what to say as he tried to hide the tube of plans behind his back. But Mr. Gedrick had a different idea. He used his pointer to poke the plans out from under Huxley's arm, and they landed in Fergus's waiting hands.

Mom and Amelia left the Airstream and joined everyone else as the plans were unrolled and pinned down on the workbench.

"These are familiar," Mom said, looking suspiciously at Huxley.

"Am I to understand that these are your plans, Elsa?" Mr. Jivins asked.

"I hate to take credit for them," she said. "They're not my best work. But yes, these are my plans."

"Hey, didn't you take a picture of this stuff in our kitchen last time you were here?" I asked.

Huxley tried his best to backpedal. "These are reproductions of work I gave Elsa to do. She might have drawn them up, I don't recall, but they were based on my ideas."

"Either way, they are far inferior to what we just witnessed," Mr. Jivins said. He ate some more popcorn and seemed to be mulling what to do next.

"Of course this new direction is even better," Huxley exclaimed, acting all excited. "I'm glad we went with option number two. I always liked it best."

"Next slide, please," Mr. Gedrick said.

I moved into the Airstream, where I pulled up a slide show file. The lights dimmed again.

"I have taken the liberty of speaking with some of your ex-employees, Mr. Harvold," Mr. Gedrick said. "Exhibit A: the Johnson Hotel. Quite a nice building."

Huxley loosened his tie. "Yes, I designed that building. Thank you."

"Actually, that's not precisely true, is it, Mr. Harvold?"

A new slide appeared with a picture of a man holding an architectural drawing. "Phillip Benderson, who worked for you five years ago. It was his first job, so of course he worked very hard indeed. These were his plans, weren't they, Mr. Harvold?"

"Well, we worked on them together," Huxley mumbled.

"All right, I'll let it slide," Mr. Gedrick said. I brought up another image. "Exhibit B."

This went on for six more examples, all of buildings Huxley had taken credit for, all done by young, up-and-coming architects who were later fired.

"This show gets more interesting by the minute," Mr. Jivins said.

Mr. Gedrick signaled for me to end the show and the lights came up again.

"It was your right to take some of the credit," Mr. Gedrick said. "You are, after all, the head of the department. But you can't have *all* the credit. Certainly not here. Not in the Darrow home. It was your intention to take full credit for Elsa's work and then fire her as well, was it not?"

Huxley's face turned red. "That's absurd! I would never—"

"Oh, but you would," Mr. Gedrick said. "You've done it many times before."

All eyes were on Huxley as he staggered backward a few steps and bumped into the workbench. "No one can make you feel inferior without your consent," Huxley stammered. It was a strange thing to say, one of his classic zingers, but it made an odd sort of sense given the situation.

Amelia got a puzzled look on her face. "Didn't Eleanor Roosevelt say that?"

"I believe you might be right," Mr. Gedrick said.

"Yup," I said from the Airstream. "Says right here, I

just Googled it. Also she's got a nice hat on."

At this point I bet all Huxley wanted to do was get in his fancy car and drive away from our house.

"How about you wait outside for me?" Mr. Jivins said to Huxley. "I'll only be a minute."

Huxley didn't have much choice. He tried to argue, but Mr. Jivins had seen enough.

When Huxley was gone, Mr. Jivins walked over to the Airstream. "You got any soda in there? I'm parched."

"You betcha!" I said. I opened a small refrigerator next to the desk and tossed a can to Mr. Jivins.

"Fresca, my favorite," Mr. Jivins said. He popped the top and drank half the can in one pull. Then he burped loudly.

"Excuse me," he said. "But my, that is good."

Everyone laughed. I liked Mr. Jivins more than ever. He seemed like our kind of guy.

Before he left, Mr. Jivins offered Mom a big fat raise and a promotion, but Mom wouldn't take it unless she could work from home.

"I wouldn't want it any other way," Mr. Jivins said. "How else are you going to mentor our future superstar?"

He looked at Amelia and smiled broadly, and she looked behind herself.

"Who, *me*?" she asked.

"Don't be so modest," Fergus said, putting an arm around my sister. "You gotta own your awesomeness."

Amelia blushed and nodded at Mr. Jivins.

"I accept," Mom said.

"We both do," Amelia said.

"Wonderful!" Mr. Jivins said.

The lights went down in the garage and the projector came back on, the plans for the community arts center on full display again.

Mr. Jivins marveled at them. He drank down the rest of his Fresca and burped again. "Now, we will build it."

Goodbye, Mr. Gedrick

We're right back where I first laid eyes on Mr. Gedrick. Do you remember that moment, in the cemetery with the leaf and the bench? Mr. Gedrick was there again, sitting in the same spot, looking at the headstone with my dad's name on it.

We looked for him all morning, but it was my idea to look here. I just knew he'd be on that same bench, waiting for us.

"I told you we'd find him here," I whispered. I looked up at Mom. "What should we do?"

Fergus and Amelia had no ideas. They didn't want to disturb him, but they were also worried about him. We all huddled together and everyone waited for Mom to decide what to do.

"How about if I go first," she said. "I'll wave you over if it's okay?"

"Good plan," Fergus said.

Everyone agreed and Mom walked out from behind the tree and slowly made her way toward the bench. Mr. Gedrick had the same green felt jacket on, the same perfectly combed hair. The wind rustled through the leaves and I felt the first chill of fall returning to the world.

"Excuse me, Mr. Gedrick," Mom said when she was only a few steps away. "Are you all right?"

He didn't turn around, but his head did rise a little, like Mom had woken him up from a dream.

"Yes, Elsa," Mr. Gedrick said. "I'm all right. And you?"

Mom went around the bench and sat down beside him.

"You loved him as much as we did," Mom said. "We all see that now. It must be sad for you, losing him."

Mr. Gedrick stared out into the cemetery and took out the field guide to the Darrows. He rubbed the cover with his thumb and looked like he was thinking of many things. "He meant just as much to me as he did to all of you."

Somehow Mom held it together, but I almost lost it. "I know, Mr. Gedrick. And I'm sorry."

We couldn't stay back anymore, so we crept up closer. We stood around Mr. Gedrick, all in a circle. I leaned in and hugged him. When I pulled away, Mr. Gedrick looked at all of us, one at a time, his bright eyes as lively as ever.

"When I arrived, I wondered if the four of you could be enough for each other. The answer turns out to be yes, and that makes me very happy indeed. Each of you was taught something different by Mr. Darrow, something you needed to be reminded of. And these things have brought you together again."

I knew what he was talking about. Mr. Gedrick had used his special kind of magic to remind us about things that were always there. All that stuff was just hidden under a load of sadness.

"But you had some work to do, too," I said. "Right?"

"Yes, Stanley. I had some work to do. Your dad was at the business of healing everyone this summer, including me. But it was the Darrow family magic that did the trick."

Mr. Gedrick rose from the bench and placed the field guide back in his jacket pocket.

"Won't you stay with us, Mr. Gedrick?" Amelia asked. "We want you to stay."

But I knew that he wouldn't. Amelia knew it, too. We all knew. Mr. Gedrick's work with us was finished. And our work on him? That work was done, too.

"I'm afraid I can't stay," Mr. Gedrick said. "But I will visit soon. How about that?"

Fergus gave Mr. Gedrick a huge hug. Everyone else joined in, surrounding Mr. Gedrick and holding him tightly.

"Are you sure you have to go?" I asked.

"Yes, I'm sure," Mr. Gedrick said. "But you'll see me again. And you'll be benching a lot more than the bar. I'm quite sure you'll even hit another Fergus fastball."

"You promise?" I asked.

"I promise."

We let him go and Mr. Gedrick began to walk. He didn't look back, not once, but he did take out his pointer and catch a falling leaf. He tossed the leaf in the air and it caught on the wind, dancing away over the graves and into the distance. I watched it fly and wondered where it would land.

When I looked back, Mr. Gedrick was gone.

The Community Arts Center

In October, the city of Chicago celebrated the ground-breaking for the community arts center. The mayor was there with a gold shovel and so were a lot of other important people. Local news outlets buzzed around with all their fancy cameras, interviewing everyone, including Mom.

"How did you come up with this revolutionary design?" a reporter asked her.

I could tell she was nervous, probably because she'd never stood in front of a camera being interviewed.

"I had a lot of help," Mom finally said. She pulled Amelia closer on one side and Fergus on the other. I mugged for the camera in front of them. "And we all had some inspiration from a special friend."

"I understand you're dedicating this project to Mr. Jonathan Darrow, who passed away unexpectedly last year. But it's also dedicated to a Mr. G.," the interviewer said. "Can you tell us anything about him?"

"That's a Darrow family secret," I said. It's pretty cool shutting down a TV reporter.

Kids ran around everywhere and their parents looked at the big signs describing the project. Everyone loved how amazing it was, and Mom shook a lot of hands. Mr. Jivins was there, too, and when he found us he gave Mom the *Chicago Tribune*.

"What an exciting day," Mr. Jivins said. "If only I had more of that popcorn and a Fresca, it would be perfect."

"Come on over for dinner and a movie," I said. "We got plenty of popcorn and Fresca."

"I'd enjoy that very much," Mr. Jivins said as he looked at Mom. I think there was some kind of spark between them, and it didn't even bother me.

"I have a ton of action figures," I said. "We could have some fun with those. Amelia calls them butt zappers, I'll explain all about that later. And I have this cool globe where we can find hidden kingdoms and stuff."

"That sounds marvelous," Mr. Jivins said.

Fergus took the paper from Mom and read the headline. "'Community Arts Center Breaks Ground, Elsa Darrow Praised for Genius Design.'"

"That sounds pretty good," Amelia said with a smile.

"It mentions you in here, too," Fergus said.

"What? No way!" Amelia said. She took the paper and scanned the story. "'A rising architectural apprentice in the city, Amelia Darrow is poised to take the Chicago skyline by storm.'"

"High praise indeed," Mr. Jivins said. "I'm glad I found you before anyone else did."

"Hey, look at this," Amelia said.

There was another story, a much smaller sidebar. Amelia read the headline: "'Huxley Harvold Fired from Senior Post at House that Elsa Built.'"

"Oh, that's just too much," Mom said.

"Not at all," Mr. Jivins said. "I insisted on that headline myself."

I looked at all the kids excited about the project. The place was buzzing with activity. I scanned the crowd because I hoped to see Mr. Gedrick. When my eyes reached the street in front of the building plot, I saw Fred pull up.

"Mr. Gedrick!" I yelled as I started running. "It's him!"

My whole family chased after me, leaving Mr. Jivins behind. We were all laughing at seeing our old friend, piling in close next to the car door.

"Let me have a look at you all," Mr. Gedrick said.

His eyes narrowed and he glanced between each of us. He seemed to be taking note of any changes in our appearance. Was he searching for any signs of slipping back into old habits? I didn't know, but if he was he'd come up empty.

"So we pass inspection?" Amelia asked.

"That you do," Mr. Gedrick answered, nodding once.

We asked him all sorts of questions about where he'd been and what he'd been doing.

"Mr. Darrow wasn't the only child I raised. There were many, many more. So I have much work to do."

Was he running an orphanage, or was he a foster parent, or was he talking about something else? He wouldn't say and I wondered if I'd ever find out.

"Next stop, Swoghollow," Mr. Gedrick said. He waved his hand in front of him and the wind picked up, blowing through the tall trees all around us. He sped away through a flurry of leaves, waving over his head.

"He sure is an interesting guy," Fergus said. "I'll never forget him."

Mom pulled all of us close as the leaves danced around us.

"He won't forget us either," she said.

We started down the wide sidewalk with the fall leaves swirling around and watched Mr. Gedrick's car disappear around a corner.

"Let's get some ice cream," I said.

"Good call, little bro," Fergus agreed.

It felt like an important summer was behind me, and a lot more were ahead of me, waiting to be found somewhere in the distance.

ACKNOWLEDGMENTS

With special thanks to the talented team of designers, editors, and marketing experts at HarperCollins. Stanley and Mr. Gedrick will never forget spending time with such a thoughtful team (and neither will I).

Ben Rosenthal, my amazing editor, offered a perfect balance of encouragement and suggestions in the search for Stanley's voice. Through five or six major edits (it felt like twenty!) Ben helped me find my way and bring this once-in-a-lifetime character to life. Bravo, Ben!

Stanley would also like to add: Hey, Veronica Ambrose, your line edit made my day!

And thank you, Katherine Tegen. You always believe in me, even when I'm a knucklehead, which is most of the time. Hug hug hug.